Wilma Tenderfoot AND THE CASE of THE Frozen Hearts

Emma Kennedy writes things for the radio and the tellybox. She also does some dressing up and pretending to be other people on TV. Sometimes she wins prizes for these things, but her greatest achievement EVER was being the Runner-Up World Conker Champion. She would have won, but was let down by a soft nut. There are two things she would like to do before she dies. 1. She would like to fly a hot-air balloon. Proper fly it, not just stare out of it like a lemon. And 2. Grow wings. That's it. She has a most excellent beagle called Poppy, who can walk like a crab. Emma's favourite word is ramalamadingdong.

Wilma Tenderfoot

AND THE CASE *of*

THE Frozen Hearts

EMMA KENNEDY

Illustrated by Sylvain Marc

MACMILLAN CHILDREN'S BOOKS

First published 2009 by Macmillan Children's Books
a division of Macmillan Publishers Limited
20 New Wharf Road, London N1 9RR
Basingstoke and Oxford
Associated companies throughout the world
www.panmacmillan.com

ISBN 978-0-330-46951-7

Text copyright © Emma Kennedy 2009
Illustrations copyright © Sylvain Marc

The right of Emma Kennedy and Sylvain Marc to be identified as the
author and illustrator of this work has been asserted by them in accordance
with the Copyright, Designs and Patents Act 1988.

1 3 5 7 9 8 6 4 2

A CIP catalogue record for this book is available from
the British Library.

Typeset by Intype Libra Limited
Printed and bound in the UK by CPI Mackays, Chatham ME5 8TD

For Melanie and also Susan

Thank you

*As always, heartfelt thanks need to be thrown
overarm into the face of Camilla Hornby,
my ever brilliant agent, but thanks of a deeper kind
need to be dropped from a height in the direction of my
editor, Ruth Alltimes — a woman so brilliant she makes
my head explode. It's been a joy.*

COOPER ISLAND

Office of the Receiver
of Burrowed Things

Hawks Brigade HQ

Is It Nearly Lunch Yet?

The
One, Small
Hill

Alan Katzin's
Aunt's House

Le Poulailler Hotel

HILLBOTTOM

Howling
Hall

poppy fields

arboretum

Valiant
Vaudeville Theatre

Cynta tree

That Place
Over There

Clarissa
Cottage

Bravura
Department
Store

new fish
freezer

COOP

MEASLY
DOWN

Doctor Kooks's
Lab

National
Museum
of Cooper

Poulet Palace

pig poke

FARSIDE

poppy
fields

Inspector Lemone's
Police Station

sheep shed

fields

cow field

Drop
Dead
Gorge

Hare Forest

beach

That Place
UnderThere

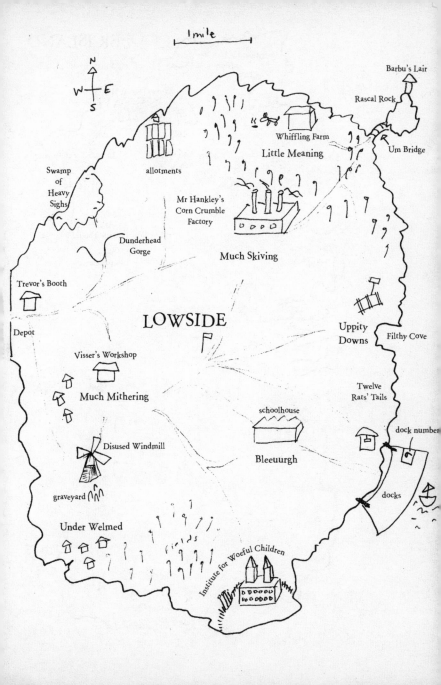

CHAPTER 1

Wilma Tenderfoot wasn't quite sure how she'd managed it, but somehow she was hanging upside down from a meat hook in the pantry. In her hand was an empty toilet roll which, although not quite as effective as a proper telescope, concentrated the mind whenever peered through with one eye. As she hung, gently swaying, Wilma was forced to conclude that maybe she didn't have this detective lark pinned down quite yet and made a mental note to remember in future not to try to climb up a rack of hams in order to investigate a theft of Madam's sausages without first taking the appropriate precautions.

Her hero, Theodore P. Goodman, the island's greatest living detective, wouldn't have got himself into this predicament, thought Wilma, taking a bite out of a particularly delicious joint of beef as she swung towards it. No. He would have done things properly and wouldn't have slipped on a slab of greasy bacon,

1

flown through the air and ended up suspended from a hook by the back of his pants.

One day, dreamed Wilma, as she rocked from side to side, she would be a great detective too and get to solve all manner of mysteries and conundrums, but for now she had an urgent problem to solve: how to get down from the rack of hams without being caught by Madam Skratch. Being an orphan at the Cooper Island Lowside Institute for Woeful Children was bad enough without being found upside down among the cold meats by the meanest matron who had ever lived.

Wilma could hear Madam Skratch's voice barking orders beyond the door. She didn't have a moment to lose. Straightening her dress and unbuttoning her pinafore pocket, Wilma pulled out a tatty heap of squashed and torn bits of paper attached by their corners to a large metal ring. Frantically thumbing through the scraps, Wilma found what she was looking for: an old folded newspaper cutting that had the words 'Theodore P. Goodman's Escape from Giant Clock' scrawled on its exterior. Opening it out as fast as she could, she examined the diagram that showed her favourite detective tied to the bottom of a massive pendulum.

'That's it!' she whispered, tapping at the picture. 'He used the pendulum to swing himself on to a ledge! If I can swing a bit harder on this ham hook, then maybe I can reach that tin of

peaches in syrup and then use the syrup to loosen up the hook and then . . .' But before Wilma had reached the end of her brilliant plan, events had taken a turn. The fabric of her pinafore had given way, and with one ripping tear she landed head first in a basket of onions. The door to the pantry swung open.

'Wilma Tenderfoot!' yelled Madam Skratch, who looked like a vulture and smelled like cabbage. 'My office! Now!'

Wilma looked up and spat a shallot out of her mouth. She was in trouble. Again.

Somewhere between England and France is an island with only one, small hill that no one has ever bothered to discover. If you go and look at a map right now, you'll be able to see it. It's just there, above that bit. It should come as no surprise that the small and ordinary-looking Cooper Island has never been discovered. Exploring is, after all, no longer taught in schools, and curiosity, the mainstay of any discoverer, has been discouraged since the unfortunate news that it can kill cats.

Hundreds of years ago the island was almost discovered by an explorer called Marco Polo. You might have heard of him. He had a beard and discovered impressive things like China and First-Class Post, so an island with one, small hill somewhere between England and France was not at the top of his To Do list. It was a Tuesday, and Marco Polo had been hard at it. 'I've

been discovering non-stop for sixteen years,' he said, standing on his poop deck, 'and in all that time I haven't had one day off. Not one.'

It was at this point that a small man called Angelo Pizza, whose daughter would invent the snack of the same name, shouted down from the ship's crow's nest. 'Ahoy!' he called. 'I can see an island with one, small hill on it!'

Marco Polo had sighed at this news and thought about how his job as a discoverer of new lands and efficient postal systems was interfering with his enjoyment of life. If you know many adults, I expect you've heard them moaning about their jobs. Well, Marco Polo was just the same. Marco Polo didn't want to go to work that day. He wanted to lie in a hammock, eat a fresh, crisp apple and have his face painted to look like a tiger. 'I can't be bothered!' he shouted up to Angelo Pizza. 'Do me a favour and just pretend you didn't see it.'

'All right!' shouted down Angelo Pizza, who carried on looking out, though he was careful not to look out again in the direction of the island with the one, small hill.

It might seem strange that no one has tried to discover Cooper Island since. But most discoverers are only interested in impressive things like the tallest mountain or the longest river. So Cooper Island, which didn't have anything that was tallest or longest or deepest, was overlooked and forgotten about and

the people who lived there were left to get on with things and mind their own business. You would think that a place ignored by the world would be a haven of calm and happiness, but you'd be wrong. Even small, insignificant islands can be hotbeds of trouble and bother, and this story is about one trouble so terrible that if you're of a nervous disposition I would advise you to put this book down immediately.

Wilma had been packing for five minutes. She had been ordered to do so by Madam Skratch after being dragged from the pantry by one ear and then yelled at for thirty-seven minutes, at the end of which the screaming matron had pulled a crumpled letter from her pocket, waved it under Wilma's nose and spluttered, 'That's it! I give up! Your tomfoolery and nonsense have tested me for the last time! You're leaving! Today!' Wilma had been surprised but quietly thrilled, an emotion that was to prove woefully misplaced. The letter was from a dried-up misery of a woman called Mrs Waldock, who had written in requesting a 'skivvy, one not too hungry nor too quarrelsome'. The unlucky wretch would go to live on the Farside of the island, where he or she would be expected to do chores like grating the dead skin off the bottom of Mrs Waldock's feet and climbing down drains to clear blockages. It would not only be Wilma's first job, but it would be the first time in ten years that she had stepped outside

the Lowside Institute for Woeful Children's front gates to go anywhere other than the obligatory Tuesday-afternoon school classes where, as well as the usual reading and writing, Wilma and the other unfortunates learned essential woeful life skills like Scraping and Scrubbing.

Wilma, who was the smallest and scrawniest of the Institute's ten-year-olds, had lived at the orphanage all her life. She didn't know much about where she had come from, only that she had been left in a tatty cardboard box at the Institute's gates during a storm so fierce that the orphanage's only tree had been split clean in two. She had been wrapped in muslin and abandoned with no further clues as to her background other than one small luggage tag tied around her neck that had three words written on it: 'because they gone'. She didn't know who had left her there or to whom the luggage tag referred. It was a mystery as deep as the seas. But one day, Wilma had decided long ago, she would find out. She may have been small, but she was very determined.

*

In the ten years that Wilma had lived at the Institute for Woeful Children she had made few if any friends. She had had a best friend once, when she was four, but it had all ended rather badly when the poor unfortunate had fallen into a furnace and been accidentally melted down and turned into a batch of spanners. Wilma quickly realized that, if she was to minimise pain and anguish in such a revolting environment, it was probably best not to get to like anyone. Instead she found her comfort in books, secreted out of the Institute's meagre library, and magazines, stolen from Madam Skratch's waste-paper basket, both filled with the to-ings and fro-ings of life on the Farside and, in particular, the adventures and triumphs of the island's greatest detective, Theodore P. Goodman. When she was young, it was the pictures of his great adventures that caught her imagination, but as soon as she could read and piece together his methods and advice, Wilma was well and truly hooked. Not only was he the island's greatest detective, he was the finest, most upstanding man that Wilma could ever imagine meeting. His noble deeds and intentions lifted Wilma from the drudgery of her everyday existence. How she longed to be a detective like him!

Every Wednesday at four, when Madam Skratch was eating cake in the turret room, and the rest of the Institute children were playing Lantha, a board game much favoured by all Cooperans, Wilma would creep down to the matron's

office and quietly pick out that week's discarded copy of *Boom!*, Cooper Island's weekly magazine for ladies of a certain age. Taking great care, Wilma would tear out the pages filled with tales of Detective Goodman's solved cases and read them over and over so that they were practically committed to memory. By learning how Theodore P. Goodman solved the island's crimes, Wilma could learn the theories of detective work and, one day, find the answers to her past. If she was going to be a detective, she decided, she would have to start practising, and she grabbed every opportunity to do so.

Once, when she was six, a large gristle pie had gone missing from the Institute's kitchen and Madam Skratch had demanded that the culprit be caught. Wilma, leaping at her first chance to have a crack at detecting, quietly decided that the pie thief had been none other than an unpredictable young lad named Thomas. His guilt, she concluded, was confirmed by the presence of flaky pastry trembling on his upper lip. But it turned out that Thomas hadn't been eating flaky pastry at all; he was experiencing a rather unpleasant attack of eczema, and as she stood having this oversight pointed out to her by a sneering Madam Skratch, Wilma discovered that hasty predictions can lead to severe embarrassments. Detection, it would appear, was a subtler art than Wilma was quite ready for.

When she was seven, Wilma, not deterred by her earlier

setback, had taken it upon herself to solve another baffling mystery. Socks were vanishing in the orphanage. Not pairs of socks, just the left ones, and Wilma was convinced that a one-legged child called Melody Trimble was the only possible suspect. But it turned out (yet again) that Wilma's suspicions were ill-conceived. Melody Trimble, as Madam Skratch exasperatedly revealed, could not have been the culprit because her one foot was a right foot, not a left. And besides, the sock thief, who had already been caught, turned out to have been a local hand puppeteer who had fallen on hard times and run out of socks. Case closed. It was another failure for the would-be detective, and one that didn't make her terribly popular. All the same, Wilma was still determined.

Then there was the time, at the age of nine, when she had tried to get to the bottom of why she, of all the Institute's Woeful Children, never seemed to get sent to a new home. Children from the Lowside Institute for Woeful children were, as a rule, farmed out to customers on the Farside of the island from the age of eight. But never Wilma. Being a curious creature, with detective-ish aspirations, she had decided to conduct a small investigation. However, because she was still not fully trained in the art of investigating, her methods were quite basic. So basic in fact that all she did was tug on Madam Skratch's sleeve and ask, 'Why am I still here, please?' But Madam Skratch answered

her with nothing more illuminating than a sharp pinch of the ear and a truck-load of onions to peel so Wilma, despite her best efforts, was none the wiser. The mystery remained just that.

But here she was, being sent out into the wider world of the island at last. She might even get a chance to do some proper detecting. The thought of it made Wilma as excited as a bottle of bees. But all that would have to wait; for now she was a Lowsider from the Institute for Woeful Children who had a battleaxe with cracked and crusty feet to meet.

In order to leave the Institute, Wilma had been furnished by the horrible matron with papers allowing her to pass from the island's Lowside to the more desirable Farside. She was allowed to take a bath, in cold water, and was handed a fresh pinafore and top shirt so that she would not 'offend the eye' of anyone with the misfortune to catch sight of her. 'Lowsiders are not welcome on the Farside of the island, and you will do well to remember it!' Madam Skratch told Wilma repeatedly, with a firm wag of her bony finger. But Wilma didn't need reminding. Every Lowsider knew that most Farsiders despised them. No one knew why. It was just the way things were.

Some children might have felt nervous and jelly-legged at the prospect of leaving the only place they had ever known, but not Wilma. She had spent too many hours staring out through

the bars of the orphanage gates, wondering what the rest of Cooper Island was like and longing to visit all the places she had seen in Madam Skratch's magazines. At the age of four, as she was tied to a rope and lowered down the orphanage well to catch frogs for supper, she had daydreamed about the sugar-cane trees that lined the Avenue of the Cooperans. At the age of five, when she was given a large spoon and told to make a statue of Madam Skratch out of chicken fat, she was so busy imagining herself posing in front of the magnificent Poulet Palace that she inadvertently gave the matron three eyes and a wonky nose, and at the age of six and three-quarters, as she was shoved up the Institute's chimneys strapped to the end of a broom to shoo away the bats, her mind flitted away to the extravagant shows put on at the Valiant Vaudeville Theatre. But most of all Wilma thought about Theodore P. Goodman and how one day, if she was very determined, he would help her find out where she had come from. In short, Wilma really couldn't wait to leave.

Given that Wilma didn't have anything much to call her own, she was ready, hat in hand and good to go, in a matter of moments. 'Tenderfoot!' yelled Madam Skratch, standing in the doorway to the dormitory. 'Have you packed your things?'

'Yes, Madam Skratch, I have,' replied Wilma with a twinkle.

'Well, hurry yourself! Mrs Waldock will be waiting. Come here and let me look at you.' Wilma trotted towards the doorway and stiffened her back, ready to be inspected. Madam Skratch towered over her and stared, tutting as her eyes darted over her grubby charge. 'You will never amount to anything,' she said, lifting Wilma's chin with a sharp finger. 'Your eyes are too green, your nose is too small, your hair is too pale and you have a mouth that is nothing but mischief. You have very little to commend you. Do as you are told, Wilma Tenderfoot, and you might have a passable life. Do not do what you are told, and your life will be a fraught and thorny misery. Do you understand?'

'Yes, Madam Skratch,' replied Wilma, tucking a wayward lock of hair behind her ear.

'And don't fidget!' snapped the matron, pursing her lipless mouth. 'I can't bear a child that wriggles. Just like a maggot! Now pick up your things and go down to the courtyard. The cart will take you to Mrs Waldock. And take this, she added, handing Wilma a letter from her new employer outlining her instructions.'

Wilma ran back to the thin and tiny bed where she had slept every night for the past ten years and picked up her small bundle of clothes. Taking care to keep her back to Madam Skratch, she reached under her mattress and pulled out her two most precious possessions: the luggage label of her birthright and a folded-up, tatty piece of paper that was now so faded it was almost wasted away. Quickly and quietly Wilma tied the label to her wrist and pressed the paper, a list of Detective Goodman's top tips for detecting, inside her bundle. She had no real need of it, of course, as she knew it by heart, and she whispered it to herself as she headed for the dorm door.

Theodore P. Goodman's Ten Top Tips For Detecting

1. Contemplate the clues.
2. Make deductions based on those clues.
3. Keep a sharp lookout for suspects and sometimes creep around after them.
4. Eavesdropping, while not encouraged in polite society, will often produce results.
5. When escaping, be circuitous.
6. Always write things down.
7. Using a disguise can sometimes be cunning (especially when things have gone a bit precarious).
8. Proper detectives always save what they're thinking till last.
9. Behave seriously at all times.
10. Never go detecting on an empty stomach.

Wilma gave a small but determined sigh. She didn't quite know what all the words meant, but one day she too would become a great and serious detective, and nothing and nobody would stop her. She took a last look around the dormitory, turned and ran towards the next chapter of her life.

CHAPTER 2

Most grown-ups are never happier than when they have someone to look down on, and the Cooper Island Farsiders couldn't have been more delighted that they had the Cooper Lowsiders to despise. As long as the Farsiders had their immediate neighbours to oppress they were saved the exacting inconvenience of recognizing their own shortcomings. Wilma had never been to the Farside of the island before, and as her cart pulled into the border station she was thrilled and frightened at the same time.

'Papers,' drawled a large, lazy-looking man in a booth. The border station was an imposing booth set between two towers. Behind it a vast wall with a huge gate in it stretched as far as Wilma could see. Everything on the Lowside seemed grey and depressed, but through the windows of the border gate Wilma was able to see green fields filled with poppies and, beyond that, in the distance, she could just make out the island's one, small

16

hill and the spires and peaks of Cooper's finest buildings. A trill of excitement fizzed through her.

As Wilma peered at the border-control buildings she had an unnerving sense of being stared at, but by whom she couldn't tell. Jumping down from the back of the cart, she handed over the envelope from the Institute. 'Work permit's in order,' muttered the border guard, who, Wilma noted from his name badge, was called Trevor. 'Stand on the red cross.'

Wilma looked down and saw a large red cross on the floor. As she stepped on to it a sudden scrape of metal sounded from the covered part of the booth in front of her. Startled, she looked up, and was even more surprised to see four sets of eyes peering back at her. Wilma didn't quite know what to do, so she just waved. On seeing this small, friendly gesture, one set of eyes blinked very hard and made a quick, sideways glance. The metal grate slammed shut again. There then followed some intense muttering that Wilma couldn't make out, and Trevor was handed a note by a mystery arm that poked itself suddenly from the wall to Trevor's left. What a peculiar place this was, thought Wilma.

'No waving,' said Trevor, reading the note. 'No waving on the cross allowed.'

But Wilma had more important things on her mind. 'Why is it,' she began, giving Trevor an inquisitive stare, 'that a person

17

is not allowed to just go from one place to another? Why does everyone need papers?'

Trevor sat back in his chair and looked a bit panicked. Another note was thrust out with some urgency. 'Humph,' coughed Trevor, scanning it anxiously. 'Because this is the Farside. And you're from the Lowside. And there it is.'

'Hmmm,' said Wilma, thinking. 'But the only difference between the two is that one side is there and the other side is here. Wouldn't it be easier to let people wander about as they pleased?'

Trevor let out a small explosive splutter. 'No, no, no!' he insisted. 'People must never be allowed to wander about. That would never do. Wander about? Goodness gracious! This is here and that is there. And that is how it is!' Another piece of paper shot out and was waved in a frantic manner. Trevor took it and read it.

'Permission to enter Farside granted, but you are being issued with an Impertinence Order.' Wilma just stared. She didn't know what an Impertinence Order was. 'Waving AND questioning . . .' mumbled Trevor, stamping an official-looking document. 'Dear me. Dear, dear me.'

Trevor then handed Wilma back her envelope of papers and passed down the stamped Impertinence Order. It was very official-looking and was in small scrawling handwriting, making

it very hard to read. Wilma held it close to her face so as to get a better look at it.

Impertinance order

*Issued by the Grand Council of Border Controls,
For suggesting that here is the same as there (which it isn't) and for gesticulating in a wild manner during government business (and putting us off), you are hereby issued with an Order forbidding you from further acts of the same here-on-in and forthwith and also etcetera.*

*Signed:
Kevin and Malcolm and Susan and IAN
(Official Border-Control Peepers)*

Wilma looked up. 'I see,' she said, tucking the Order into her pinafore pocket. 'Well, that's that. Can I go now?'

'No. Now you have to wait for an appropriately long and unnecessary length of time. Read the sign,' said Trevor, pointing towards a poster. Wilma turned and looked at it. There it was. Item number four on the list of Border Control Procedures: 'Lowsiders will be required to wait for a long and unnecessary

length of time until such time as Border Control decides it has been long and unnecessary enough.'

Wilma shook her head. This place was mad. Still, she didn't want to get herself another Impertinence Order so she went and sat in the back of the cart and hoped for the best.

Two hours and thirty-three minutes later, Trevor decided that Wilma's wait had been sufficiently long and sufficiently unnecessary. 'You can go through now,' he said with an official nod. Wilma was quite tempted to do something rude, like stick her tongue out at him, but given that she seemed to be in enough trouble already she thought the better of it and just stuck her tongue behind her front teeth instead.

Wilma's first glimpse of the island's Farside was wondrous. As the cart pulled through the border gates and the fields of poppies rose to a crest Wilma was treated to a grand view: to the south, the rolling plains of farmland that melted into a deep forest; to the north, the one, small hill, at the base of which nestled the town of Hillbottom; and before her, the capital town of Cooper, which seemed so grand and so sparkling that Wilma could do nothing but bump along with her mouth open.

Used only to the drab surrounds of the Institute's bleak walls and dead and dusty gardens, Wilma was struck by how colourful everything was: people wore bright-coloured suits of purple

and green, hanging baskets filled the air with scent, and shop windows, far from being empty and dour, were packed to bursting with produce and treats.

But none of this wonder was meant for Wilma. Beneath the hazy facade of easy living there ran a grimy seam of underlings and servants, all of them Lowsiders, who made the Farside spick and span for their employers to enjoy. Wilma was not meant for a life of laughter or bubbles: Wilma was at the mercy of her new mistress. The cart stopped with a jolt.

'Howling Hall – you're here,' mumbled the driver, throwing Wilma a glance over his shoulder.

The Waldock house was a towering wooden turret with a wonky top, a bit like a wizard's hat worn at an angle. The windows were grimy, black with dust and mould, and the steps to the front door were overgrown with weeds and scratchy thorns. As the cart slouched away through the gates Wilma stared up at her new home, her heart sinking. This was worse than the Institute. Oh, well. She'd just have to make do and mend. It probably only needed a good clean, she decided, rolling her sleeves up.

Holding her letter of introduction in one hand, Wilma took her first steps towards the house. The front door burst open. Wilma jumped. Framed against a dim and dingy light there stood a woman, fleshy like a toad. Flecks of spittle were gathered at

the corners of her mouth, and her eyes peered out through fatty slits. It was Mrs Waldock, Wilma's new employer.

'Are you the girl?' bellowed Mrs Waldock, in a voice that sounded like wet sponges being thrown into buckets.

'I am, ma'am, yes,' said Wilma, taking care to throw in a curtsy.

'Don't look like much,' barked back Mrs Waldock, giving her a once-over. 'Scrappy thing, ain't you? Can you lift? Can you mend? Can you jump over a five-bar gate using only one hand?'

Wilma blinked. She wasn't quite certain how to answer. 'I'm not sure,' she replied, scrunching her face up. 'But I can touch my nose with my tongue. Look.'

Mrs Waldock stared at Wilma as she licked the end of her nose. It was impressive – even she had to accept that. 'Well, get in then,' said Mrs Waldock, belly shuddering as she gestured inside. 'Take your things down into the cellar. Through that door. To the left. Those are your quarters. Leave your things and then come back up to the parlour. I have an errand that needs running.'

'Here's my letter of introduction,' said Wilma, holding it out as she entered. 'Madam Skratch at the Institute told me to give it to you.'

Mrs Waldock licked the spit from her lips and snatched the letter from Wilma's hand. Unfolding it, she read aloud:

Dear Barbara,

The child that has handed you this letter is called Wilma Tenderfoot. She is ten years old. She is of reasonable character but has a tendency to daydream and mutter. If you find her staring off into the middle distance, just shout her name once, quite loudly, and that should do the trick. Please feel free to beat her. You may have your own preferred methods of punishment, but I have always found a few thwacks with a Naughty-Boy Belt (brochure attached) to yield the best results. As for feeding her, she will do quite well on one meal a day and will be perfectly happy with scraps or leftovers.

As you know, we offer a full thirty-day trial free of charge. If you are satisfied with Wilma (and we're sure that you will be), then we will send you an invoice for her purchase at the conclusion of the trial period. Should Wilma not meet your requirements, please return her in a cardboard box and we'll be happy to replace her. In the event of Wilma being killed or severely mutilated during the trial period, then we will ask you to pay the fee in full. This is merely to cover our own costs. I hope you understand.

It just remains for me to thank you for choosing the Institute for Woeful Children and we hope you are happy with our product.

I remain,
Deborah Skratch

'Humph,' slobbered Mrs Waldock, tossing the letter on to a sideboard. 'I certainly shall NOT be paying if you get yourself killed or mutilated. So make sure you don't!'

'Yes, Mrs Waldock,' replied Wilma, who didn't have to make much of an effort to hope that THAT didn't happen.

CHAPTER 3

The inside of Howling Hall was no more welcoming than its exterior. Dark, heavy furniture brooded in corners, and patches of damp mould crawled up the walls. One weak and fizzing light did its best to cut through the gloom, but it was like throwing a pea to stop an elephant. Wilma grimaced. This place was awful.

The cellar, which would be Wilma's home for the foreseeable future, was covered in spiders' webs and smelled of wet rags. Wilma sighed and threw her bundle down on to a small mattress on the floor. So this was it. It would be impossible not to say that she was experiencing something akin to bitter disappointment, but Wilma, though small, was a determined girl, and she was ready to make the best of things. As she strained to peer into her dank, dark surroundings, Wilma decided that if she cleared this bit here and tidied up those things over there then it wouldn't be so bad after all.

A small snuffle sounded from a corner. Wilma froze. It is a general truth that when in gloomy, damp circumstances, the last thing you want to add to your troubles is a sudden noise from an unknown source. But having decided that the absolute worst-case scenario was an un-tethered crocodile, and then having concluded that that was surely impossible, Wilma mustered up her last scrap of inner strength and peered deep into the depths of the hole where the noise had come from. There it was again! Bending down to get a better look, she reached out with her hand and was surprised to find something a little bit warm and a little bit wet. Suddenly two large, brown eyes were looking at her. Wilma stood back, a little startled, but then, sensing that she was in no immediate danger of being eaten, she bent down again. 'Come on,' she said gently. 'Come out. I won't hurt you.'

Out from the murky corner stepped a raggedy and much neglected dog. He was small in stature, as high as Wilma's knees, and had floppy ears, one of which was crumpled and tatty. His eyes were large and pleading and his mouth downturned, as if he was in a permanent state of melancholy. With his tail between his legs and his head bowed, he crept forward. He was in such a sorry state that as Wilma looked down at him she had to struggle not to cry. Quickly untying her bundle, she extracted the remains of a piece of ham she'd been given for the journey and

held it out. The beagle, for that's what it was, smelling the food, wagged his tail a little and came closer to take it. As he ate he looked up into Wilma's eyes, and at that moment Wilma knew, for the first time since she was four, that she might have found someone who, at that moment, needed a friend just as much as she did. 'What's your name?' said Wilma, kneeling down to give the dog a stroke. There was a small dull disc hanging from his collar. Wilma took it between two fingers and read it. 'Pickle!' she said, smiling. 'Your name's Pickle.'

Pickle wagged his tail even harder. Sometimes it's hard to put your finger on the exact moment when lifelong friendships take flight, but as the two of them sat on that dirty mattress in the middle of the cold, damp cellar there was no doubt that Wilma and Pickle had just become best friends.

The errand that Wilma had to run for Mrs Waldock was a simple one. 'I want two buns – one iced, one with currants, from Mr Hankley, the baker,' drooled Wilma's mistress. Having given Pickle a sneaky wash and rub down in the overgrown garden, Wilma set off from Howling Hall with the dog at her heels and a spring in her step. It was evidently the first time Pickle had been clean since arriving as Mrs Waldock's guard dog two years previously – not a job he seemed to have been doing particularly well. In fact, when he first appeared from the cellar beside Wilma, Mrs Waldock seemed a little startled and less than impressed that the dog was still living with her at all. It was only Wilma's reassurances that he would make a very handy housegirl's assistant that persuaded her new mistress to let him stay. Pickle had huffed with relief as Wilma finished cleaning him up, and Wilma had been pleasantly surprised to discover that what she had thought was a grey and dingy-coated mutt was actually a golden-brown hound with white paws and tail tip and a sleek black saddle patch on his back. 'Dare I say it,' said Wilma, as they walked towards the bakery, 'but you're a very handsome dog!' Pickle looked the other way coyly when Wilma said this, because everyone knows that dogs can't take compliments.

During their brief outing two things of significance took place. First, as Wilma ran out through Mrs Waldock's gates she bumped into a small man clutching a helmet with a lamp on it.

'I'm very sorry, sir,' Wilma apologized and ran on. That man was called Alan Katzin and he was about to go potholing, but we'll learn more about him in a minute.

The second thing that happened was on Wilma's return. As she and Pickle dashed back towards the house Wilma skidded to a halt and stood rooted to the spot with her mouth open. In front of her was standing a man smoking a pipe with his hands in his pockets. Nothing odd about that you might think, except the man was well known to Wilma, very well known indeed.

'Theodore P. Goodman,' she whispered as he turned and entered the front gate beside him. Wilma's new home was next door to Cooper Island's greatest living detective!

But enough of that. Let's get back to Alan Katzin, who, within seventy-two hours of bumping into Wilma, was going to be stone-cold dead. How very ghastly.

CHAPTER 4

Alan Katzin was a creature of habit. Every year, without fail, he would pack his knapsack and take the Cross Island Cart to Hillbottom, the village where his aunt lived. Alan Katzin was not overly fond of his aunt. It wasn't because Alan Katzin's aunt was mean or had dry, clacky lips. The problem with Alan Katzin's aunt was that she had unnaturally smelly feet. Not only that, but in the evenings she liked to put her feet up in front of the fire and twiddle her toes which, as far as Alan Katzin was concerned, just made the matter worse. But there was something that made putting up with his aunt's unnaturally smelly feet a small price to pay: Alan Katzin's aunt baked incredible lemon meringue pies and made astounding pickled onions and Alan was obsessed with them. He ate so many of his aunt's pies and pickles that she had a hard time keeping up. In the world of Business, this is called Supply and Demand, and in Alan Katzin's

aunt's house the Demand was greater than the Supply. On the morning that Wilma bumped into Alan, it was this discrepancy that set in motion a chain of events that would, three days later, leave Alan Katzin and his aunt done in, murdered and dead.

It was 11.34 in the morning and Alan Katzin had already managed to eat five lemon meringue pies and forty-seven pickled onions. As he sat at the table in his aunt's kitchen Alan noticed something unusual. Wiping the last crumbs of lemon meringue pie from his lips, he turned to his aunt and said, 'I've noticed you've got linoleum on the wall and wallpaper on the floor, aunt. Shouldn't that be the other way round?'

Alan Katzin's aunt, who was sitting at the other end of the table folding tea towels, looked up and said, 'Yes, Alan, you're right. Normally you would put the linoleum on the floor and the wallpaper on the walls, but I have unnaturally smelly feet and I find that walking on wallpaper rather than linoleum makes them sweat less.'

Alan Katzin's eyes widened ever so slightly when he heard his aunt speak with such candour about her foot-odour problem and at first he didn't know how best to respond. Then, being very careful not to blink or look away, Alan gazed back at his aunt and said, 'Have you? I've never noticed.'

Of course, as we already know, Alan had noticed his aunt's unnaturally smelly feet because it was impossible not to, but he

quite rightly realized that there was nothing to be gained from pointing out an embarrassing personal problem to someone who already knows they have it. Alan Katzin's aunt, on hearing that someone might not have been aware that she had unnaturally smelly feet, felt happy for the first time in her life. She smiled and her nose crinkled up to her forehead.

'Alan,' she said, standing up and undoing her apron, 'I'm going to pop down to the grocer's and buy some more ingredients to bake another batch of lemon meringue pies. It'll only take an hour or two until they're ready. While you're waiting, why don't you go out and explore the one, small hill?'

'Yes, Aunt,' said Alan Katzin, nodding and looking out the window. 'It's a lovely day. In fact, I might even go for a pothole. I haven't done that in ages.'

'Good idea, Alan,' said Alan Katzin's aunt, smiling. 'And I'll go and get those ingredients. I never knew a fellow so overly fond of lemon meringue pie as you!' And with that, she pulled on her overcoat and left the cottage. Alan Katzin stood and watched his aunt go and, for a moment, as he stared after her, he realized that, despite the smell, he was overly fond of her too.

If you've ever been out walking with a grown-up through a field or sitting with one in a garden, you will often hear them moaning. Grown-ups moan all the time about a great many

things, but there's one thing that's guaranteed to drive them mad. 'Look at that,' the grown-ups will say, pointing and shaking their heads. 'Molehills!' Grown-ups think molehills are caused by moles coming up for air, but they're not. They are breathing holes for potholers, and portals to adventure.

Alan Katzin knew this, and as he wandered the lower slopes of Cooper's one, small hill, it wasn't long before he found a row of perfect molehills. Knowing that this meant a secret tunnel was somewhere about, Alan stood as tall as he was able, put both his hands above his head, took a deep breath and dived into one of the holes. There was a deep and endless smell of mud and roots, and as Alan Katzin crawled further in his fingers became wet and sticky. The tunnel had become so dark that Alan couldn't see the end of his nose so, taking a match from his pocket, he reached up to his helmet with the lamp in the middle of the brim and lit the candle inside, sending a dull, white beam out in front of him.

It was at this point that Alan Katzin's life became destined to be a short one. In the light of his lamp, something was shining right back at him, and Alan, who had no idea that the gleaming rock was going to be the death of him, reached down, picked it up and got out his rock hammer.

Holding the parsnip-shaped mass in one hand, Alan tapped the bright seam that ran down its centre. With one strike, the rock crumbled into bits, and there, among the dust, was the biggest and most beautiful single jewel that the quiet man from Cooper had ever seen. Alan's eyes widened. This was big. This was VERY big. Alan Katzin gulped. 'Crikey!' he whispered and then, unblinking, added a little excited, 'Ooooooh.'

There was no doubting it. The discovery of this rock was a life-changing event, and as Alan Katzin scrabbled back out of the molehill and ran down Cooper's one, small hill he had time to reflect. Does this mean I'm rich? he thought to himself, skipping over a heather bush. 'I could buy a suite at the island's poshest hotel, Le Poulailler! I could buy the hotel! I could buy the island!' he yelled, hurdling a cluster of daffodils. But as his feet touched the ground, he skidded to a halt. 'Hang on,' he said, fingers resting on his lips. 'I don't even like the hotel. I just like lemon meringue pies and pickled onions. What am I going to do with a fortune? I'm a simple man. With simple tastes.'

Alan Katzin looked into his hand. The stone was cold and hard. Thrilling things sometimes come with a terrible responsibility, and as the gentle soul stared down he suddenly realized exactly what he should do.

'Are you quite sure, Alan?' asked Alan Katzin's aunt after she had sat down with the shock of it.

'I am, Aunt,' said Alan Katzin, who had placed the extraor-

dinary jewel in the middle of the kitchen table. They both sat, staring at it as it emitted a glow so intense that the tops of the freshly baked batch of lemon meringue pies looked as if they were made of solid gold. 'I'm not a rich man, but I'm not a poor man either. And what would I do with all the money that selling it would bring? I might be able to live in a mansion or take up a suite at Le Poulailler, but I just like lemon meringue pie and pickled onions and coming to stay with you for my holidays. That's all I need. No, this belongs to everyone. I'm going to give it to the Museum, and knowing that everyone on Cooper will be able to enjoy it is reward enough.'

Alan Katzin's aunt thought her nephew was quite mad, of course, but Alan had made his mind up. He was giving the jewel to Cooper.

CHAPTER 5

Jeremy Burling was the Cooper Island Receiver of Burrowed Things. He was a tidy, organized fellow who was very fond of making lists. Every day, as he strolled down the gravel path to his office, he would make a list in his head of the things that needed doing. On that day, Jeremy's list was as follows:

1.
2.
3.

In short, Jeremy Burling didn't have the slightest inkling that he was about to have the most exciting day of his life. On a normal day Jeremy would think about his list, get the office keys out of his pocket and twirl them on his finger as he approached the door. But on that day he didn't, because there were two people

waiting at the end of the path before him. And Jeremy didn't know who they were.

'Excuse me,' said Alan Katzin, who was standing with his aunt at the office entrance, 'are you the Receiver of Burrowed Things?'

'I am, yes,' said Jeremy, coming to a stop and standing a little taller.

'I'm Alan Katzin. And I've found something,' said Alan, his eyes brightening.

Inside Jeremy's office, Alan put his rucksack up on the counter, reached into it and pulled out a bundle of tea towels. Peeling back the layers slowly, Alan revealed the most wondrous and most enormous gem ever found.

Jeremy Burling had a keen eye for all things precious and wasn't given to expressions of great surprise or alarm. All the same, he found himself saying, 'I have never seen anything like it, Alan,' as he pulled out a pair of double-lens microscope glasses so as to have a better look. He peered at the jewel and then, looking up with an expression of not inconsiderable shock, said, 'And I have no idea what it is!'

Alan Katzin's aunt squinted her eyes up a little. 'It's a very big and very precious stone,' said she. 'Even I know that.'

'Yes,' said Jeremy Burling, fixing Alan Katzin's aunt with a

small stare. 'I'm aware of that. What I mean is, I don't think this is something that's ever been found on Cooper Island before. If I'm right, Alan, you've found a brand-new and very precious stone. Imagine that!' But Alan Katzin couldn't imagine that, so he just stood with his mouth open to pretend that he could.

'But let's not get giddy,' said Jeremy, folding his double-lens microscope glasses back into his waistcoat pocket. 'I'm going to run some tests. Put it through the Gem Discoverer. That's a machine that recognizes the carbon compounds of all the precious stones. It'll give me a reading of how high the carbon content of this stone is. That number will correspond to this chart.' Jeremy pulled on a string to his left and a poster rolled down.

Alan Katzin nodded and wished he'd paid better attention during carbon-content classes at school, but he hadn't so there it was.

The Gem Discoverer was a spherical ball that seemed to be made of nothing more than an intense blue light, set between silver clamps, inside a small glass case. As Jeremy placed Alan Katzin's gemstone between the two needles of the clamp, the blue sphere fizzed and sparked. With the gemstone suspended inside the sphere, Jeremy turned some dials and the unit whirred into activity. The sphere began to rotate, slowly at first, but with

each turn it spun faster and faster until the gemstone looked like a liquid blur. 'It won't take long,' said Jeremy, tapping the countertop with his fingers, but it did. 'Not much longer now,' said Jeremy, tapping more impatiently. 'Nearly done,' he assured them, looking confused. Eventually a short, sharp ping sounded. 'Aha!' said Jeremy. 'The moment of truth!'

A round coin-like disc slid out. Jeremy Burling picked it up and looked at it. 'Seventy-three,' he said out loud. 'Your gemstone has a carbon content of seventy-three, Alan.'

'Is that good, Mr Burling?' asked Alan.

'I think it might be better than good, Alan,' said Jeremy, pulling the carbon-content chart back down and looking at it. 'I think it might be nothing short of incredible. Look at that. According to the carbon-content chart, there is no known gemstone with a carbon content as high as seventy-three. Do you know what that means, Alan?'

'Yes, Mr Burling,' said Alan, but he was lying, because he hadn't paid any attention to that subject at school, as has now been well established.

'That's right, Alan!' said Jeremy, eyes beaming. 'You have discovered a brand-new extremely precious and extremely massive gemstone!'

Alan Katzin's aunt was so overwhelmed that she wanted to jump up and down, but, given that her unnaturally smelly feet

were extra smelly after the long walk from the cottage, she thought better of it and just waved her hands in the air instead.

'I'm going to have to report this to the Minister for Massive Finds, Alan,' said Jeremy, who was very excited. 'But before I can do that,' he added, leaning over the counter, 'you have to name it.'

Alan Katzin was gripping the bottom of his cardigan as if his life depended on it. 'Name it?' he asked. 'Like a baby?'

'Sort of,' said Jeremy, smiling. 'It's a scientific tradition. Whenever anything new is discovered for the first time, the person who finds it gets to name it.'

'It's the most precious thing in the land, Alan,' said Alan Katzin's aunt, 'so choose carefully.'

'Can I call it lemon meringue pie?' asked Alan, because that was the most precious thing he could imagine.

'Not really,' said Jeremy, scratching his neck. 'Think it through.'

Alan wondered if he could call the jewel pickled onions but realized that sometimes not saying thoughts out loud is probably for the best. 'Can I call it Alan?' asked Alan.

'Hmmm,' said Jeremy, who had also decided not to say out loud what he was thinking right at that moment. 'What about your surname? Katzin – that's got the right sort of ring to it.'

'And it's the most precious thing I can think of,' winked Alan Katzin's aunt, giving her nephew a little nudge.

'All right then!' said Alan, nodding and smiling. 'Katzin it is!'

And so it was that the most precious jewel ever found was named the Katzin Stone. And from that moment on, the happy aunt and her nephew were doomed.

CHAPTER 6

The day that was to be Alan Katzin and his aunt's last was the day the Katzin Stone was being transported from the underground vault of the Office of the Reciever of Burrowed Things to the Cooper National Museum. The honour of escorting the Katzin Stone fell to Captain Brock and the 2nd Hawks Brigade, a crack team who specialized in watching things very closely.

'The Katzin Stone is here,' said Captain Brock, pointing to a square on a blackboard that had the word VAULT written under it. All the members of the 2nd Hawks Brigade nodded and made notes in their leather-bound Mission Books. A Mission Book is a book that you make important notes in about things you mustn't forget, especially if you don't want to lose your job.

'And it will be travelling, by rail,' said Captain Brock, tapping his finger along a dotted line on the board, 'to here,' he added, pointing at another chalk square that had the word

MUSEUM written under it. 'Our job is to watch it,' said Captain Brock in a voice that suggested he meant more business than usual, 'and ensure that none of the island's Criminal Elements get their hands on it.' Captain Brock stared at the 2nd Hawks Brigade who all stared back at him. 'You might want to write that bit down,' said Captain Brock, staring at the 2nd Hawks Brigade a little harder.

As the brigade scribbled away, Captain Brock tapped his hands together behind his back. Anyone who knew Captain Brock knew that this meant he was thinking harder than when he was thinking about unimportant things like crispy bacon or warm sand between his toes. Captain Brock was thinking about the island's Criminal Elements and about what a terrible thing it would be if the Katzin Stone fell into their clammy hands.

Meanwhile, back in Hillbottom, Jeremy Burling was making sure that everything was shipshape and above board. The Katzin Stone was safely under lock and key until it was ready to be moved, and the Receiver of Burrowed Things was adamant that nothing would jeopardize its safety. So when Jeremy heard the familiar tinkle of the front-door bell, just after Captain Brock had arrived ahead of his men, he was right to feel suspicious. Given that the closed sign was up, and given that it was a very special and very dangerous day, Jeremy couldn't help but feel a short, sharp stab of anxiety. Likewise, Captain Brock clasped his hands even more tightly behind his back. The island's Criminal Elements could strike at any moment. But they needn't have worried. 'Oh thank goodness!' Jeremy said, when he saw who it was. 'Alan! Hello! Come in!'

'I'd like to see the Katzin Stone, please,' said Alan, who was a little taller than Jeremy Burling remembered.

'Certainly,' replied Jeremy. 'Do you have the special pass I gave you?'

'Oh yes,' answered Alan, holding it up for Jeremy to look at.

Jeremy was surprised that Alan didn't seem especially pleased to see him, but it was a tense day for all concerned and short tempers were to be expected. Although Jeremy Burling wasn't meant to show the Katzin Stone to anyone except Captain Brock, he didn't think twice about taking Alan Katzin down to the vault. After all, it was Alan who had found the stone in the first place and he *had* been given a special pass. 'Very nice,' said Alan, in a slightly deeper voice than Jeremy remembered, as he examined the open box, the stone glittering within it. 'Very nice indeed.'

'Have you got a cold?' Jeremy asked.

'Yes,' said Alan, rather quickly. 'It's come on suddenly and appears to be a very bad one.' And he coughed as if to emphasize the point.

'Best get out of this damp vault then,' smiled Jeremy. 'I'll lock the vault but leave the box open for Captain Brock to see it. Then I'll seal it away for good, ready for travel.'

'Yes,' said Alan passing the box back and putting one hand in his pocket, 'lock it away. Why don't you do that?'

'Oh!' said Jeremy, putting a hand to his forehead. 'You must think me very rude. I've offered you nothing. Actually, I've got some lemon meringue pie in my office! Would you like some?'

'No, thank you,' said Alan. 'I'd better be going.'

Jeremy looked puzzled as he waved off Alan, who seemed to be in a great rush, but he thought no more about it. After all, he had to make sure that the Katzin Stone reached the Museum without falling into the hands of the island's Criminal Elements. And that was far more important than eating lemon meringue pie.

At 12.04 precisely, Captain Brock's crack team of the 2nd Hawks Brigade arrived outside the Office of the Receiver of Burrowed Things. Two soldiers to the left of the building, another two posted to the right. Captain Brock, because he had the most experience, watched in both directions at once. Please don't try this at home. Captain Brock has been specially trained to watch things very carefully and you have not. Trying to look in two directions at once can result in a nasty headache or

instant death. 'Please note that I am seeing no Criminal Elements to the left or to the right,' said Captain Brock, tapping his hands together behind his back. 'I will now proceed into the Office of the Receiver of Burrowed Things, where I will watch the Katzin Stone being taken out of the vault.'

Most vault doors are made of solid steel and this one was no different. 'Would you mind not watching while I tap in the code for the vault door?' Jeremy asked Captain Brock. Captain Brock frowned. *Not* watching something did not come naturally to him, but he understood that these were exceptional circumstances so he averted his gaze and instead watched a drop of water as it slid its way down the vault's slimy walls. 'I've tapped in the code for the vault door,' said Jeremy, after a series of clicks. 'You can stop not watching now.'

Captain Brock's forehead relaxed and he looked back at the vault door, which was now open. Inside the shadowy vault was an open small metal box. Captain Brock stepped forward and made sure he was looking as hard as he possibly could. Jeremy lifted the box into the light. 'The Katzin Stone, Captain Brock,' he said, with a sense of awe.

Captain Brock felt the breath catch in his throat. The Katzin Stone was, without a doubt, the most beautiful and most enormously precious thing he had ever been asked to look at. 'This must never fall into the hands of the Criminal Elements,' said

Captain Brock with an ever greater sense of purpose. 'Please lock the box and take it out of the vault. You will be escorted on to a train where you will take the box to car number five. You will sit in a designated chair, where the crack team and I will stand in a circle and watch you and the box all the way to the Museum. Do you understand?'

'I do. Thank you, Captain Brock,' said Jeremy, who suddenly sounded very serious, like when adults are discussing garden furniture.

No one spoke during the three-mile trip. Jeremy had quite wanted to chat about how the weather had been unusually pleasant for the time of year and the fact that he could see bluebells in the fields but, realizing that Captain Brock and the 2nd Hawks Brigade were standing round him in a circle and staring so hard they were breaking into a sweat, he thought better of it. There was a time for idle chit-chat, but this was not it.

As the train pulled into the Museum station Jeremy stood up. 'Gently does it, Mr Burling,' said Captain Brock, maintaining eye contact with the box at all times. 'Hawks – two of you stay with the box, two of you out on to the platform.'

'All clear!' shouted a soldier from the platform.

'Proceed, Mr Burling,' said Captain Brock, and out they all went from the train.

*

Standing on the platform was the Welcoming Committee from the Museum. As Jeremy stepped down on to the train platform the Museum Curator, a very fat and pompous gentleman, motioned to a man with a trumpet who, on cue, blew a fanfare. 'Stop that at once!' yelled Captain Brock, still staring at the box. 'Do you want to alert our presence to every Criminal Element in Cooper?' The herald stopped blowing on his trumpet and looked a bit disappointed.

'Captain Brock,' said the Curator, 'do you have the Katzin Stone? Is it secure?'

'It is, Mr Curator,' said Captain Brock, inching towards the Welcoming Committee.

'Then let us see it,' said the Museum Curator, puffing out his chest to show everyone that he was not to be meddled with.

'Here you are, Mr Curator,' said Jeremy, handing over the box. 'The Katzin Stone.'

The Curator smiled and took the box into his hands. He let out a little sigh and opened it.

'Saints preserve us!' cried Captain Brock.

The Curator looked up, his face ashen and drawn. 'Gentlemen,' he said, his puffed-up chest deflating, 'the Katzin Stone has gone!'

48

*

And at that precise moment, in the village of Hillbottom, a scream rang out as the neighbour of Alan Katzin's aunt found her and her nephew lying on the wallpapered floor of the kitchen, done in, murdered and dead.

CHAPTER 7

The peppermint tea was almost how Theodore P. Goodman liked it, but Mrs Speckle knew better than to take it in until the colour was just right. The detective's peppermint tea needed to be the colour of spring grass: any lighter and he would complain that it was too weak, any darker and there would be an afternoon of frowns that Mrs Speckle could well do without.

Mrs Speckle, Detective Goodman's housekeeper, was unable to bear the cold. Quite why this was, nobody knew, but even on the hottest summer days Mrs Speckle would be wrapped in woollen jumpers and woollen trousers, with not just one but two woollen bobble hats (for good measure) on her head. From her heavy duffel coats to her underpants, everything that Mrs Speckle wore was knitted. Even her wellington boots.

As she stood waiting for Theodore P. Goodman's peppermint tea to turn the correct shade of green, she pulled her second

bobble hat a little further down her forehead. There was a sharp chill and she cast her eyes about to see where it might be coming from. Mrs Speckle had a phenomenal talent for pinning down the source of draughts, and as she scanned the room she took in everything that might be the culprit. Perhaps the draught was coming in through that hole in the wall where that ant and his large extended family seemed to have moved in? Mrs Speckle pushed the butcher's block away and bent down to have a look. Nope. No draught there.

As Mrs Speckle straightened she noticed that the edge of the curtain that hung over the back window was trembling. Taking hold of the fabric with one hand, she pulled it aside and realized that the left side of the window had wriggled itself ajar. Mrs Speckle frowned, stretched her arm across the counter and tried to get a grip on the window's handle, but the awkward angle prevented her. She leaned back into her knitted wellingtons and wondered what she was going to do next, and as she did she heard a small voice coming from the other side of the window.

'Is this where Theodore P. Goodman lives?' said the voice.

Mrs Speckle peered in the direction of the voice but could see no one. All the same, she said, 'Yes,' because if there was one thing she knew for certain, it was that answering voices that seem to be coming from nowhere is always best.

'Theodore P. Goodman the famous detective?' said the voice, a little excited.

'Well, what other Theodore P. Goodman is there? Of course it's the famous detective.'

'Has he got an apprentice?' asked the voice.

'What is this?' asked Mrs Speckle, pushing open the window suddenly and impatiently. 'It's not my job to be answering questions about my employer and whether he has or has not got an apprentice, which he has not. Especially when you can't see who's asking them. Apprentices indeed!'

A small face appeared at the window. It was Wilma and she was beaming and wide-eyed. 'Does he really live here? Really truly? I live next door. I used to live on the Lowside at the Institute for Woeful Children, but I've been sent to work for Mrs Waldock. So far I've seen a baker's shop with a giant cake, a broken swing and a bush in the shape of an eagle. I've read all about Theodore P. Goodman. I'm going to be a famous detective too. My name's Wilma. This is Pickle. He's a dog. Aren't you hot, wearing all those knitted things?'

Wilma, as we know, was only ten years old, which goes a long way to explaining not just her dizzy demeanour but her sudden lapse in manners. Mrs Speckle, on the other hand, was fifty-two years old and was in no mood for explaining her love of knitted things to a cheeky young girl. Or her dog. 'Listen to me, young lady,' said Mrs Speckle with a marked tug of her bobble hat, 'famous detectives get to be famous detectives by hard graft and indulging in long periods of contemplative silence which, on the present evidence, I suspect you will find impossible.'

'What does contemplative mean?' asked Wilma, hooking both her hands over the frame of the opened window and swinging on it.

'Thinking about something very hard,' said Mrs Speckle. 'Which I think you should do before you swing on that window again.'

'Who's swinging on my window, Mrs Speckle?' asked a voice like a warm sponge with hot liquid chocolate at its centre. Puddings, like people, can be serious, and for this reason you will sometimes hear adults saying, 'This is a serious pudding.' Well, this voice was a serious voice, and at the sound of it Wilma fell off the window and into some snowdrops. Pickle barked and leaped about a bit. Mrs Speckle, who had noticed that the peppermint tea was turning a shade of green that was not the right kind, winced and spun around. There, standing before her, was Theodore P. Goodman.

Let's make no bones about it – Theodore P. Goodman was a very impressive man. As a descendent of the great Hayten Araucan, one of the founding fathers of Cooper Island, the

detective was allowed to wear a moustache. The dense fawn whiskers that gathered under his nose fanned out to stunning, blonde peaks with the tips a deep brown as if they'd been dipped in treacle. His hair was the colour of wheat, and his head, as it caught the sunlight coming in through the window, looked as if it was made of gold. He wore a waistcoat made from the finest silk and a battered leather overcoat that had pockets deeper than oceans. There was a chain attached to one buttonhole, at the end of which hung a magnifying glass, the tool of choice for any detective worth his salt.

'Mr Goodman!' said Mrs Speckle who was still staring at the peppermint tea and wishing that her employer would drink it before everyone's day was ruined. 'Nothing for you to concern yourself with. Look now, here's your tea. Shall I fetch you a few corn crumbles to go with it?'

Theodore's moustache twitched at the mention of corn crumbles, for which he had a terrible weakness, but he was a detective first and biscuit lover second, and if someone was swinging on his window he wanted to know who. 'You were conversing with someone, Mrs Speckle,' said Theodore P. Goodman, fingering his magnifying glass.

'What does conversing mean?' said a small muffled voice from outside the window.

'Talking, chatting and generally entering into conversa-

54

tion with,' said the detective poking his head out of the back kitchen window.

When people whose lives are going to be forever entwined meet for the first time, they have no way of knowing how important they are going to be to each other, and as Theodore P. Goodman, who was a very famous and serious detective, met Wilma Tenderfoot, who was a very young and cheeky Lowsider, there was no way of knowing that within just one week Wilma would be in such perilous danger that Detective Theodore P. Goodman would be her only hope. But for now Wilma wasn't in perilous danger; she was just lying in a famous detective's snowdrops which, although not life threatening, still spelled trouble.

'Hmmm,' said Theodore, eyeing the small child. 'It would appear you have crushed my snowdrops.'

'I didn't do it on purpose,' gabbled Wilma. 'I'm not lying here because I'm tired. Or because I wanted to ruin your flowers. I was swinging on your window. And I fell off. I think I've cut my hand,' added Wilma, holding up a small bloodied finger.

Mrs Speckle rolled her eyes. The peppermint tea was quite ruined and, as if that wasn't bad enough, there were now minor injuries to be dealing with. Pushing herself up as high as she could, given that she was wearing flat knitted wellington boots, the housekeeper tried to get a look at Wilma's cut finger, but it was no good. She was too short, and her first and second bobble hats had now slipped so far down her forehead that all she could see was wool. Theodore, noticing that his housekeeper was getting into a heavy-set muddle, put a hand on her shoulder. 'It's all right, Mrs Speckle,' said he. 'I'll fetch her in. And besides,' he added, looking into the pot in front of him, 'that peppermint tea is the wrong side of right. I know it and you know it, but if I never taste it, I shan't remember it. So if I fix up our young visitor, then you can fix another pot. And a few corn crumbles will do very nicely. Thank you, Mrs Speckle.'

Even though this solved all manner of current difficulties, Mrs Speckle was a stubborn old lady not given to instant acts of forgiving and forgetting, and as she shoved her two bobble hats back up her forehead and set about making another pot of peppermint tea she mumbled something under her breath that some grown-ups might take exception to. With that in mind, and given that soft eyes are watching, it's in nobody's interests to repeat Mrs Speckle's words here. Let's just say she was cross and leave it at that.

As Theodore stepped out into the side garden of Clarissa Cottage, which was the proper name of the house in which he lived, he looked down and saw Wilma still lying in his flower bed and holding her bleeding finger aloft. Next to her was

sitting a crumpled-looking beagle. Theodore P. Goodman did not have younglings of his own as he was not married. He had been engaged once to a dancer called Betty but, well, the less said about that the better. So as the famous detective stared down at the little girl, he wasn't quite sure what to do. Theodore was used to daily dealings with the island's Criminal Elements, who were burly fellows with poor personal hygiene and wonky teeth, but when it came to small, cheeky children he had little, if any, experience. 'Yes, well,' said Theodore, looking at Wilma over the top of his mighty moustache, 'this won't do. Up you get and follow me.'

Wilma's finger was stinging, and if she'd had a mother who had kind eyes and comfy arms she would have cried that very instant but as she followed the famous detective into Clarissa Cottage, and saw the short, sharp look that Mrs Speckle gave her, she realized that crying wouldn't get her anywhere. Besides, Wilma was so thrilled to be actually inside the house of Theodore P. Goodman that her stinging finger was almost forgotten.

'I've come from the Institute for Woeful Children. I'm going to be a detective,' said Wilma, trotting to keep up with Theodore, who was striding ahead of her.

'Really?' said Theodore, to be polite.

'I am,' said Wilma. 'I expect I'll just solve the larger cases. You know, murders and . . . some more murders.'

'Hmmm. In here, please,' said Theodore, gesturing into a large bathroom. Theodore P. Goodman was not a man used to the chitter-chatter of small girls. He wanted to fix this young child's finger, send her on her way and sit down to a nice cup of peppermint tea and a plate of corn crumbles. In short, as far as he was concerned, a serious detective and a girl from a Woeful Institute had no business being friends. None at all.

'What a big bathroom!' exclaimed Wilma. In the far corner there was a round bath so grand it was elevated from the floor with steps going up to it. Above it were three arched windows that blazed with sunshine, while the floor was a mass of tiny coloured tiles. 'Hang on a minute!' she said, cocking her head to one side to get a better view. 'Look at the floor, Pickle! It's a map of Cooper Island!'

Pickle barked. Not because he understood what a map was, because he didn't. He's a dog. But because he quite liked all the new smells.

'That's right,' said Theodore, opening a cupboard above the sink. 'It's called a mosaic.'

'Mosaic,' said Wilma, looking down and nodding. 'That's the fourth new thing I've seen today.'

Theodore smiled and pulled out a small stool that was kept next to the laundry basket. 'Sit here, please, and hold out your finger,' he said, pushing the stool towards her.

'Who's that?' asked Wilma, sitting and pointing at a photograph that was hanging on the wall. The photograph was in black and white and was of a young boy standing next to a grave-looking gentleman who was wearing an expression that said, 'Not today, thank you,' which is something adults say when people they don't want to be bothered by try to bother them. Theodore, who was unwrapping a cotton-wool ball, cast a glance over towards the wall.

'Well now,' said Theodore, 'the young boy is me. And the gentleman was a very great detective called Anthony Amber. He taught me everything I know.'

'Were you his apprentice?' asked Wilma, spinning round to stare the detective square in the face.

'Yes, that is correct. Hold out your finger, please. I can't clean it if it's being waved here, there and everywhere.'

'So does that mean you came from the Lowside, like me?' asked Wilma, eyes widening.

'No,' said Theodore, giving her a small smile, 'I'm afraid I'm very much from the Farside. But I don't really hold with all that Farside, Lowside business.'

'So who's your apprentice?' asked Wilma, fixing Theodore with an unblinking gaze.

Sensing where this was leading, Theodore concentrated on cleaning the blood from the end of Wilma's finger. He

dropped the cotton-wool ball into a bin to his left and un-ravelled a length of bandage. 'I don't have an apprentice,' he said eventually, realizing that Wilma was still staring at him.

'That's a bad business,' said Wilma, shaking her head and pursing her lips together, 'but I can start today. So that's that problem solved. I mean, I'll have to do my chores for Mrs Waldock, but I'm sure I can spare you a few hours.'

Theodore dropped the bandage on the floor and frowned a little. Bending down to pick it up, he wondered how he had got himself into this mess and how he was going to get himself out of it. He was well used to telling people bad news about ghastly thefts and gruesome murders. That was part of his job. But telling small girls bad news about hopes, dreams and job prospects was something else entirely. Still, thought Theodore, it's always best to be honest and straightforward so, wrapping Wilma's finger with the bandage, he looked right at her and said, 'I'm not looking for an apprentice right now, thank you. Keep your hand up.'

Wilma blinked. 'But you will need one soon?' she asked with a plaintive look. 'Because I only live next door. I know I'm not a detective yet, but I have got some experience. Like last week, at the Institute, a bag of barley sugars went missing from Tommy Barton's desk and no one knew who'd done it, but I worked out it was Frank Finley because when I was talking to him his mouth was full of sweets.'

'That must have required a great deal of deduction,' said Theodore with a small smile.

'What's deduction?' asked Wilma. The word rang a bell. 'Isn't that when you do sums but take away rather than add? What's that got to do with Tommy Barton's barley sugars?'

Theodore tied the ends of Wilma's bandage in a knot. 'Deduction,' he explained, 'is the word used for sums when you take away rather than add. That is correct. But in this context it means working something out after examining a series of clues.'

Wilma stared at Theodore. 'What does context mean?'

Theodore made a small noise in the back of his throat. 'Context means the situation in which something exists. So in the context of sums, deduction means taking one number away from another. In the context of crime, a deduction is the solving of a clue based on the facts. So in the case of Tommy Barton's barley sugars, the fact that Frank Finley was discovered with a mouth full of sweets is a clue that could lead to the deduction that it was he who was the culprit. Culprit means person who did it.'

Wilma nodded. 'Oh yes, I remember. Deductions. It's number two of your top tips for detecting. And contemplating is number one! Does this mean I'm your apprentice now, because being an apprentice means you learn stuff from someone who knows what they're talking about?' Theodore stared back at Wilma. 'That is what I have deductioned,' said Wilma, looking very serious.

'Deduced, not deductioned,' said Theodore. 'I don't need an apprentice now; neither am I looking for one soon. Well, your finger is all cleaned up and fixed so I expect you can run along, and you might want to stop your dog eating that bar of soap.'

'All the same,' said Wilma, hopping down from the stool and taking Pickle by the collar, 'if you are looking for one, then I expect I'm the person you're looking for.'

'Hmmm,' said Theodore, holding the bathroom door open. 'You remember the way out, don't you? Goodbye.'

'Thank you for fixing my finger, Mr Goodman,' said Wilma, walking past him and remembering the manners she had forgotten earlier.

Theodore had run out of things to say at this point, but in any event his eye was following the woollen-clad figure of Mrs Speckle, who was walking towards them with a tray of peppermint tea and corn crumbles. Balancing the tray on one arm, she opened a door to the left of the corridor. As Wilma passed it she peeked in and stopped in her tracks. 'Is that your study?' she asked, in a squeal of excitement.

'It is, yes,' said Theodore, who was looking over Wilma's

head at the plate of corn crumbles that Mrs Speckle was lifting off the tray.

'Can I look in it?' asked Wilma.

'No, you can't,' said Mrs Speckle, coming back out of the study. 'You've bothered Mr Goodman enough. Off you go. Inspector Lemone is here, Mr Goodman. About the Katzin Stone being stolen and two poor souls killed over in Hillbottom.'

Something stolen? Two people murdered? Wilma had to think fast.

Theodore nodded and tucked his fingers into the top of his waistcoat pockets. 'Send him in, Mrs Speckle.'

'Come on, you two, off you go,' said Mrs Speckle, from behind Wilma and Pickle, wiping her hands on her knitted apron.

'Oh!' said Wilma. 'I just remembered! I left my scarf in the bathroom!'

Mrs Speckle sighed. She had to fetch Inspector Lemone, hang out the washing and get herself to the baker's before it shut. She looked at Wilma.

'All right,' she said. 'Go and fetch it. But be sure to get yourself home after that, you hear?'

'Yes, Mrs Speckle,' said Wilma who had no intention of doing any such thing . . .

CHAPTER 8

Inspector Lemone was a stodgy fellow whose cheeks looked like buns. He was a bit out of breath because Clarissa Cottage was a good forty minute walk from the police station and the Inspector, who had no interest in physical exercise, was very out of shape. Normally an inspector would have a sergeant or a constable who could drive them around on the back of a bicycle or in a fancy carriage, but Cooper only had one police officer and Inspector Lemone was it. He was on his own and at the mercy of sharp inclines.

As Mrs Speckle returned to the front hallway Inspector Lemone was feeling in his pockets for a handkerchief to wipe his forehead, which was damp with sweat, but as he heard her coming he abandoned his search, and quickly wiped his brow with the sleeve of his mackintosh instead. After all, he didn't want Mrs Speckle to know he couldn't walk for forty minutes

without breaking into a sticky mess. The fact that Mrs Speckle was a widow and that the Inspector had had a soft spot for her for over ten years is nothing to concern us here. This isn't a story about soppy romance, it's a story about murder and stealing, so don't give that piece of information a second thought.

'Mr Goodman says you can go through now, Inspector,' said Mrs Speckle, picking up the basket of just cleaned washing that she had left on the side table.

'Thank you, Mrs Speckle,' said the Inspector who watched as she picked up the basket. 'Can I help you with that?' he added, removing his hat and holding it in his hands.

'No, thank you,' said Mrs Speckle, oblivious to the Inspector's attentions. Inspector Lemone tried a small smile but Mrs Speckle wasn't even looking. Oh, what was the point?

The Inspector had been at Clarissa Cottage many times over the years and so knew his way to Theodore's study. As he turned and walked up the long corridor from the hallway he heard a small noise. Because it was so small, he couldn't be quite sure what it was or if he had even heard it at all. 'Hello?' he called out, peering into the darkness. 'Is anyone there?' He stood very still for a few moments, which he enjoyed because it was so physically undemanding, but he heard nothing further. The Inspector shrugged his shoulders and opened the door to Theodore's study.

Theodore P. Goodman's study was a treasure trove of criminal matters. One wall was so covered in awards and certificates and diplomas that diplomas were hanging on certificates and certificates were hanging on awards. There were bookshelves and glass display cases and photos everywhere. By the fireplace were two brown leather armchairs and a small table laid out with a marble Lantha board. Theodore was sitting in one of the armchairs, saucer in one hand and a cup of peppermint tea in the other. As the Inspector sat down Theodore anxiously noted that Mrs Speckle had only brought in two corn crumbles so, with his mouth full of hot peppermint tea, there was little he could do but watch as Inspector Lemone picked up both biscuits and popped them into his mouth. Theodore gulped. 'Hmmm,' he said, staring at the empty plate. 'Perhaps I'll just ask Mrs Speckle if we might have a few more corn crumbles.'

'She's hanging up washing, Goodman,' said the Inspector, wiping his mouth with the back of his hand. 'Shame. They are awfully nice, aren't they?'

Theodore managed a weak smile and put down his cup and saucer. 'So, Inspector . . . to business. The Katzin Stone?'

'Here's the thing, Goodman,' began Inspector Lemone, flipping open a small notebook that he had pulled from the inside breast pocket of his mackintosh, 'the Katzin Stone, the most

valuable jewel ever found, was stolen from places unknown somewhere between the Office of the Receiver of Burrowed Things and platform 3B of the Cooper National Museum train station some time between o-twelve-hundred hours and o-thirteen-hundred hours and twenty-five minutes.'

'You don't say the "o" when the number is over nine, Inspector. That's how the twenty-four-hour clock works. You can say, "o-seven-hundred hours" but you can't say, "o-ten-hundred hours", or, "o-eleven-hundred hours". The "o" is for numbers lower than ten.'

'I know that,' replied the Inspector, looking up. 'I just like saying the o bit. It sounds more official.'

Theodore said nothing, but raised his eyebrows.

'Obviously an inside job,' sighed the Inspector. 'I've arrested Jeremy Burling, the Receiver of Burrowed Things. So far, he's saying nothing.'

'Hmm. I shall have to speak to him, of course. Arrange that for me, please, Inspector. And what of the people who died?' asked Theodore, picking his pipe out of his waistcoat pocket and filling it with rosemary tobacco. 'What's the connection?'

'Alan Katzin and his aunt.' Inspector Lemone nodded. 'Katzin found the stone. Took it to Burling. We can only assume that Burling did them in too.'

Theodore stopped packing his pipe.

'And were they killed before or after the Katzin Stone was stolen?'

'Hard to say. We think it was about the same time.'

Theodore stood up and walked towards the door of his study. 'Inspector,' he said, glancing back, 'we must get to the Museum at once. But first, you,' he added, opening the door with a flourish, 'had better get back to your mistress, where you belong.' Wilma, who had had her ear to the keyhole and had heard everything there was to hear, looked up. 'Do you know the expression "Caught in the Act", young lady?' asked Theodore, looking down. Wilma shook her head and shifted on her feet. Pickle, who was sitting behind her, rolled over and waved his legs in the air, a tactic that had often got him out of scrapes, but Theodore was unimpressed. 'It means being caught doing something that you shouldn't. So that's another new thing you've learned, which I think you'll agree is more than enough for one day. Inspector, if you please, we haven't a moment to lose.'

'We're not walking, are we?' asked the Inspector, standing up and following the great detective out through the door.

As Wilma watched Detective Goodman and the Inspector sweeping down the corridor she felt quite certain that as far as learning new things today was concerned, there was plenty of

room for improvement. If only she knew the way to the Museum. But then she remembered. 'The mosaic!' she whispered, shooting an excited look at Pickle, and off she ran to get her bearings.

CHAPTER 9

Wilma was on her hands and knees. She had found the You Are Here arrow on the bathroom floor to the left of the sink and was tracing the snakelike path with her bandaged finger down from Clarissa Cottage to the big village of Coop. The post office was under the towel rack and the baker's was next to the soap stand. If she followed the road past the Poulet Palace, which was to the right of a small rag-roll rug, then all she had to do was turn left at the toilet brush and the National Museum would be directly in front of the laundry basket. Brilliant. With her bearings all found, Wilma stood up and took one lingering glance at the picture of the young Theodore with his mentor, Anthony Amber. 'Come on, Pickle,' she said, with a sense of resolve. 'We need to hurry. If we don't, we're going to miss everything. Nothing and nobody stops Wilma Tenderfoot.'

*

'Oh no,' said Inspector Lemone, as he looked at the tandem bicycle that Theodore was wheeling out from his side-garden shed. 'Can't we take the steam train, Goodman? It runs on the hour.'

'Yes, Inspector, the train does run on the hour,' said Theodore, taking the seat at the front, 'but it is now just past the hour, so we would have to wait fifty-seven minutes for the next one to come along. Therefore, we ride on the tandem. Put this protective hat on and tuck your trousers into your socks.'

Theodore tossed over a scuffed green hard hat, which the Inspector caught and stared at unimpressed. 'Green doesn't suit me,' he said, looking up at Theodore, who was holding a far more thrilling black hat.

'Well,' said Theodore, understanding perfectly what the Inspector was getting at and ignoring it, 'it is a difficult colour.'

There is nothing worse than having to wear something you don't like, and the Inspector was quite anxious that a certain housekeeper didn't see him wearing the horrible green hat. 'We're not riding anywhere near your washing line, are we, Goodman?' he asked, looking about with some anxiety.

Theodore raised an eyebrow and said nothing. If he had been a flighty man stirring the pot of romance stew then it might

have been different. But he wasn't. He was a famous and serious detective, so he looked at the Inspector and said, 'The National Museum, Inspector. Time is of the essence.'

'Shhhhhhh!' whispered Wilma to Pickle as they crept into Mrs Waldock's back kitchen. 'We mustn't wake her up.' Mrs Waldock, having enjoyed her mid-morning double-bun snack, was slumped in a chair and snoring. Somehow, Wilma had to get to the Museum as quickly as possible. But how?

Wilma, despite always being determined to make the best of things, had been forced to conclude that life at the Waldock residence was not as rosy as it might have been. First there was the damp and smelly cellar; second, there was the house itself: dusty, dark and brooding; and third, there was the bizarre manner in which Mrs Waldock communicated Wilma's instructions for the day. Every morning since Wilma had arrived, a letter had landed on the doormat addressed to her. She had never received a proper letter in her life and she couldn't help wondering, as she carefully opened the first envelope, whether it was something exciting, like an invitation to go kite flying or a wild-card entry into that year's Lantha Championships. Sadly it was not. The letter was from Mrs Waldock and it outlined her chores for the day:

Today you will do the following:

1. *Pluck the hairs from my chin*
2. *Scrape the scabs from my elbows*
3. *Remove the bogies from my nostrils*
4. *Muddy the windows and smear the floors*
5. *Chop wood (but under no circumstances light a fire)*
6. *Sharpen the knives (in case of intruders)*

Every day for the last three days a new letter had arrived, and each morning Wilma had found herself with a list of revolting and maddening chores. It was something of a mystery that Mrs Waldock should be so miserable and contrary. After all, thought Wilma, she was a Farsider, for whom life should be an endless burst of sunbeams, but here she was shut up in the gloom and stuffing herself with the very worst that Cooper cuisine had to offer. What Wilma didn't know, of course, was that there was a reason for Mrs Waldock's cantankerous nature. It is a universal truth that ladies who stop pulling up their socks and start growing a moustache have generally given up on things. The root cause – an unspeakable let-down of a romantic nature that leaves the rest of one's life as joyless as a crate of broken eggs. Someone, somewhere, had once broken Mrs Waldock's heart, but as to who, or why, there was very little to go on.

The only clue to Mrs Waldock's past was a large leather travelling chest that sat gathering dust in one of the upstairs bedrooms. On Wilma's second day at Howling Hall, one of her chores had been to sweep up all the half-bitten toenails from the bedroom floors. Being a curious and determined little girl, Wilma, intrigued by the oversized trunk, had felt compelled to open it and have a good peek. 'It's not snooping,' she explained to Pickle, who was sitting watching her. 'It's investigating, which is a different thing entirely.' Given that everything at Howling Hall was drab and grey, Wilma was astonished to find a mass of dazzling and sparkling costumes. There was also a poster for a circus glued into the lid. She made a mental note to think about it again when she was a proper detective.

But, remembering the trunk at that moment, Wilma suddenly knew how she was going to get to the Museum . . .

The National Museum of Cooper had won the Most Brilliant Building on the Island Award every year since it was built. As Theodore and Inspector Lemone freewheeled down the Avenue of the Cooperans the grand entrance plaza stretched out in front of them. Larger than a football pitch, it was surrounded by sugarcane trees that visitors to the museum came in their hundreds to lick. Younglings queued up to chew the sweetest trees, and Sugarcane-Swizzle vendors stood on every corner

cutting down the sticky twigs and leaves and pulping them into delicious bubbly drinks. Beyond the plaza was the Museum, a six-tiered pyramid that held all the treasures of Cooper. Inspector Lemone couldn't have been more relieved as they came to a stop. 'I'm exhausted, Goodman!' he said, getting off the tandem and leaning against the wall of the Museum with one hand.

'It was downhill all the way, Inspector,' said Theodore, dismounting neatly. 'The sensation you are experiencing is not one of exhaustion but the burst of exhilaration that riding at speed can provide. But don't worry – they are easily confused.'

Inspector Lemone wiped away the sweat on his forehead for the second time that day and stared after Theodore P. Goodman as he marched towards the Museum entrance. 'No,' he muttered to himself. 'Believe me. I'm exhausted.'

There will always be individuals who are naturally athletic. You know the sort: they glide rather than galumph, they float rather than flop, and they can throw things overarm without looking really, really rubbish. Inspector Lemone was not one such individual and neither was Wilma who, having borrowed a pair of skates from Mrs Waldock's mysterious trunk, had managed on her journey to the National Museum to knock over three post boxes, a bin and a five-year-old called Susan. It was like watching a baby deer on a pogo stick. Out of breath and panting, Wilma crashed to a stop in front of the grand plaza, with Pickle, his skinny frame bouncing along, ears flapping in the wind, at her heels.

The place was packed. The theft of the Katzin Stone had been in the after-lunch papers, and citizens had come from all over the island to stare at the empty display case and say things like 'It's an awful shame' and 'How terrible', because everyone, no matter how much they deny it, loves a notorious case of thievery. 'Sorry!' said Wilma, as she skated into a family from That Place Over There, a small village on the west of the Farside. 'Excuse me!' she said again, as she glided over the toe of a woman from That Place Under There, a village to the south. All countries have someone whose job it is to give everywhere its proper name. In Great Britain, for example, the task of naming places first fell to a man called Gregor Thellred. He was very good at what he did and came up with great place names like Plymouth and Ipswich. Sadly for Cooper, their place namer was a scruffy and disinterested lad called Brian whose lack of imagination was breathtaking, and as a result there are villages on Cooper called terrible things like Bleeuurgh, Little Meaning and Isitnearlylunchyet.

Looking about frantically, Wilma couldn't see the detective anywhere, but as she skated closer to the main gates she caught sight of a stodgy police officer puffing his way across the square. 'Inspector Lemone!' cried Wilma but, just as she kicked down

with her left skate, she felt a hand tightening round the back collar of her pinafore.

'No skating allowed on the plaza,' said a raspy voice. Wilma looked up into the face of an angry-looking man in uniform.

'You don't understand,' said Wilma, trying to wriggle herself free. 'I've got to get to the Museum. It's the Katzin Stone and—'

'No skates! And the queue for the Museum starts over there,' said the attendant, indicating a line of people snaking away from the entrance. 'From there,' he went on, pointing at the end of the queue, which was so far away Wilma couldn't even see it, 'your waiting time will be four hours.'

'But you don't understand!' shouted Wilma. 'I have to get in there now! I'm helping Theodore P. Goodman crack a very important case.'

'You? Help Theodore P. Goodman?' asked the attendant, looking down his nose at the young Lowsider. 'I don't think so. But even if you are, you're not going anywhere with those skates on.'

'All right! All right!' said Wilma, holding her hands out. 'I'll take them off. But Mr Goodman will hear about this, you know,' she said, giving the man one of her special stares. 'You are preventing me from all manner of contemplations and deductions.' She unstrapped her skates.

'The end of the queue is the other way,' said the man, as Wilma set off towards the entrance gates.

'I knew that,' said Wilma and, keeping one eye on the man, she turned and headed in the direction of the Avenue of the Cooperans, Pickle hard on her heels.

As soon as Wilma reached the first sugarcane swizzle tree she stopped and ducked behind it, yanking Pickle alongside her. Pretending to chew its sugary bark, she peeped out from behind the gloopy trunk to see whether the attendant was still watching. But her luck was in: a group of opticians on a work outing had been standing in the wrong queue for over an hour and were looking for someone to blame. They had the attendant surrounded and all of them were shaking their fists at him. One optician was so cross he knocked off the attendant's cap, which set in motion a chain of events that could only be described as ugly. Wilma's heart was beating fast. She had to get inside the Museum! 'But how?' she wailed. 'That queue goes on forever!'

Pickle nudged at her with his nose and made a snorting noise in the direction of a cart that had just pulled into the square. 'Of course!' Wilma exclaimed. 'It's delivering a Tyrannosaurus rex skull! I read about it in Mrs Waldock's mid-morning paper! We can creep over, jump inside the skull and get in that way! Pickle! You are brilliant!'

Under normal circumstances Pickle would have felt a little embarrassed at the compliment, but even he had to agree that riding anywhere in a massive bone was probably the best idea he'd had in ages.

CHAPTER 10

'Can't make head or tail of it, Goodman,' said Captain Brock, who had been pacing at the far end of the gallery. 'I saw the stone at the Receiver's office. Stayed with it all the way. Get to the station, it's vanished.'

'It must have been Jeremy Burling.' The Curator nodded, gripping the top of his cane. 'But how did he do it? And more importantly, where is the stone?'

'Burling swears blind he had nothing to do with it,' puffed Inspector Lemone. 'We've searched his office and his home. Can't find a thing. Only two other people were given passes into the vault: Captain Brock and Alan Katzin.'

'This is a disaster for the Museum, Mr Goodman,' said the Curator, thumping his cane on the floor. 'A disaster!'

Theodore twitched his moustache and pondered. The Harlequin Gallery was on the fifth floor of the Museum. It was a

round room with no windows, but the gloom was punctuated by three illuminated display cases containing the greatest treasures of Cooper. In the case to Theodore's left there was a large golden egg, in the display case to his right there was an ancient alabaster Lantha board set with azure-blue pieces, a five-sided dice and intricately carved playing squares, and in the centre of the room the case where the Katzin Stone should have been stood bare. 'Greed,' began Theodore, leaning in to look at the empty display case, 'is a dangerous mistress.'

'Quite right,' answered the Curator, with a solemn nod. 'Even the greatest of men can be turned by its charms.'

'Succumbing to charm is man's fatal weakness,' said a lady clad in black, sashaying towards them. She was a striking woman: dark hair tied up in a tight bun, with one wayward curl creeping down her cheek, deep brown eyes that smouldered below a high fringe and lips as red as tomatoes.

'Ahh, Miss Pagne!' said the Curator, gesturing towards her. 'I don't think you've met. Theodore, this is my new assistant. Started last week.'

'A fine time to be joining the museum, Miss Pagne,' said the great detective, holding out his hand. 'Theodore P. Goodman. A pleasure to make your acquaintance.'

The fingers of Miss Pagne's hand curled about the detective's, her crimson nails flashing in the dim light of the displays. 'No

need for introductions, Mr Goodman,' she purred, fixing Theodore with a wry smile. 'Your reputation precedes you.'

'I'm a Lemone,' said the Inspector, holding out his hand, only to have Miss Pagne ignore it. 'I mean I'm an inspector. Inspector Lemone. Not an actual lemon. Yes. That's who I am.'

Miss Pagne turned her velvet-brown eyes towards him and mustered a weak smile.

'Now then, Mr Curator,' continued Theodore, ignoring his friend, 'I would like to look at the box in which the Katzin Stone was stored.'

'I have it,' said Captain Brock, handing over the silver container. 'I've been staring at it for hours. There's no secret panel. Nothing.'

'Interesting,' muttered Theodore, taking the box and peering inside it. 'Hmmm. Slight odour. Just as I thought. Captain Brock, are you quite sure that you saw the Katzin Stone inside it?'

'If any other man asked me that question I would strike him down!' blustered Captain Brock, bristling. 'When I say I have seen something, there can be no doubt that I have seen it. To suggest otherwise is slander, sir.'

'Forgive me, Captain Brock,' said Theodore, with a small bow. 'I should have phrased my question with greater care. I have no doubt that you saw what you thought was the Katzin

Stone, but my question is this: was it ever the real Katzin Stone?'
Captain Brock looked more puzzled than an undone jigsaw.

'What are you getting at, Goodman?' asked the Curator,
placing both hands over the top of his cane.

'I mean, Mr Curator, that the stone that was transported to
the Museum under Captain Brock's care may have been a fake.
And that the real Katzin Stone was already gone.'

'How do you come by that, Goodman?' said Inspector Lemone, having to wipe his brow with the effort of thinking.

'If the real Katzin Stone had been in this box upon its collection, then I suspect Alan Katzin and his aunt would still be alive.
They needed to be out of the way to allow access to the stone.
The man that took the stone was dressed exactly like Alan. He
would have needed his clothes and the pass into the vault. I'd bet
my boots on it.'

'Then where's the stone that I saw?' asked Captain Brock,
tapping himself in the chest with an angry finger. 'Where did
that go?'

'Simple, Captain Brock,' said Theodore, taking out a handkerchief with a flourish. 'The stone inside this box was designed
to disintegrate, and here,' he added, picking out something from
inside, 'is the proof.' The Curator, Captain Brock and the Inspector leaned in to get a closer look. Pinched in the folds of
Theodore's handkerchief was a gleaming shard.

84

'Well, I never,' said Inspector Lemone. 'If you haven't done it again, Goodman!'

'Done what?' said a small voice behind them. 'Have I missed much? No matter. Just carry on as you were.' Everyone turned round. Wilma waved at them. 'Only me,' she said, and grinned. 'Came in inside a big dinosaur's skull. It was quite cramped. But he liked it,' she added, as Pickle licked his lips.

'No, no, no,' said Theodore, with a frown. 'This won't do. Wilma, does Mrs Waldock know that you're here?'

'If I said not really, would that be a problem?' said Wilma, twisting the edge of her pinafore in her fingers.

The detective fixed her with a serious stare that left Wilma in no doubt that she might be in considerable trouble. 'I shall have to take you back when I'm done,' he said. 'Now stay close to Inspector Lemone and not one peep out of you. Do you understand?' Wilma nodded and smiled up at the Inspector.

Captain Brock had taken Theodore's handkerchief and was holding the shard to the light. Wilma gasped a little as she saw it. 'It's like sunshine,' she said.

'Not one peep, remember?' said Inspector Lemone, putting a finger to his lips.

'What is it, Goodman?' asked the Captain, squinting at the sparkling object. 'And how did it disintegrate?'

'Look inside the box, Captain,' said the detective, holding it

out for everyone to see. 'There's a tiny hole in one side. The clasp of the box was designed in such a way so as to release a melting agent when the box was shut. It is my belief that the fake Katzin Stone was made of nothing more than coloured sugar, and that when the box was closed a concentrated gas or liquid simply melted it away.'

'Devilish simple,' said Miss Pagne, smiling a little.

'So the person who took it,' said Wilma, wide-eyed, 'must have swapped the stone! Or swapped the box! Like in that magic trick when you were solving the Case of the Vanished Buttons. I've got it on my Clue—'

'Shhhhhh, Wilma,' whispered the Inspector, giving her a nudge.

'She's quite right,' acknowledged Theodore, raising an eyebrow, 'if a little overexcitable . . . so we may be looking for someone with an exceptional ability for sleight of hand.'

'Though why swap it for a stone that melted?' asked the Curator, shooting Wilma a sideways glance.

'Except for that shard. And thank goodness for it. By examining it I shall be able to determine exactly what it's made of. When I understand that I'll be nearer to knowing who made it. Clearly whoever it was wanted something that would leave no trace – but buy him some time.'

'But what about the real Katzin Stone, Mr Goodman?' said

the Curator, tapping his cane on the floor. 'It's all very well you chasing theories but the most precious jewel ever found is still missing. And I want to know what you're going to do about it.' He took a step forward to emphasise his point and, catching his foot on the edge of one of the display cases, slipped a little and fell against the Captain. The gleaming shard, the detective's only clue, flew out of the soldier's hand and into the gloom of the gallery. It was impossible to see where it had gone.

'We must find that shard!' shouted Theodore. 'Everyone tread very carefully!'

Wilma couldn't have been more thrilled. If she put her mind to it, she might actually be able to help with a case. She looked down at Pickle. 'Come on,' she whispered, 'get sniffing. We need to find it!'

'Nothing over here!' cried out the Inspector.

'I'm seeing nothing,' yelled Captain Brock. 'Light! We must have light!'

Wilma, who still had the skates around her neck, suddenly remembered something. 'When Mr Goodman solved the Case of the Unlit Match,' she whispered to Pickle, who had his nose firmly to the ground, 'he found a silver doorknob by bouncing light off his magnifying glass. Light is always attracted to light, Pickle!' With that, she unhooked the silver skates from her shoulders and held them out in front of her. At first, she saw

nothing, but suddenly, as she waved the skates around and down to her left, they seemed to pick out the smallest of glimmers. Wilma nudged Pickle and pointed towards the tiny twinkle. Pickle, snaffling up every smell in the vicinity, gave a small but definite yelp, turned and bounced on his front paws. Following Pickle's encouragement, Wilma got down on to her knees and reached her hand into the dark gap between two of the display cases. Feeling with her fingertips, something cold and sharp came into touch.

'I've got it!' she yelled, jumping up. 'Look! I've found it!' Wilma held the shard in her fingertips and looked at it. It so reminded her of caramel that she couldn't resist raising it to her mouth. 'What's the point of taking it all the way back to Mr Goodman's house just to find out if it's sugar? I'll eat it now! I'll be able to tell you if it is!' Wilma shut her eyes and lifted the shard to her lips, but as she did so she felt a hand dashing it from her fingers.

'No, Wilma!' shouted Theodore. 'It may be poisoned!'

'But you said it was just sugar, Mr Goodman!' stuttered Wilma shakily.

'Sugar that might have been dipped in a chemical compound,' said Theodore, with a stern frown. 'Though I can't work out why – if it was meant to have disappeared completely. An insurance policy perhaps . . . Still, smell the edges.' He lifted up the

broken shard in his hand. Wilma leaned towards it and sniffed. A foul, pungent smell flooded her nostrils and she recoiled.

The Curator had heard enough. 'The Katzin Stone stolen. Two people murdered. A young girl almost poisoned. Who could be so despicable as to do such a thing?'

Theodore stared hard at the empty display case. 'I don't know, Mr Curator. But I'm going to find out.'

'Probably someone with very bad manners, I expect,' opined Wilma with a nod; a deduction that everyone could agree with.

CHAPTER 11

Barbu D'Anvers was a very bad man: short fellow, russet suit, golden waistcoat and a heart as black as evil. If you lived next door to him, you'd move. He had no friends and no one ever sent him birthday cards. Everyone who ever met him hated him, even nuns. And they like everyone. That's how bad he was. Like all very bad men, Barbu had an evil lair. And like all dreadful dens, Barbu's was situated at the top of a malevolent-looking crag. His crag was called Rascal Rock and it protruded from the main island like a stuck-out thumb. For anyone intending to devote their life to wrongdoing, it's very important to adhere to the following golden rule: 'Location, location, location', and Barbu, of all the island's Criminal Elements, had the very best spot from which to manage his mischief. At the top of Rascal Rock, Barbu's house was perched like a black crow ready to peck out the eyes of anyone who came

calling. And to come calling, they first had to cross the very narrow and slightly precarious Um Bridge. He didn't get many visitors.

Ever poised to capitalize on the island's misfortunes, Barbu was pacing in his study.

As he strutted back and forth across the room laughing, Tully, who had the unfortunate task of being Barbu's Right-Hand Man, tried to laugh along. 'Tully,' guffawed Barbu, 'has there ever been a more Brilliant Criminal than Barbu D'Anvers?'

'Is this another trick question?' said Tully, reaching into his waxy overcoat for a corn-cob cigar. 'Ummm . . . not sure . . . yes?' He ducked too late as Barbu turned on his heel and threw a marble statuette, which bounced off the side of Tully's head.

'No, Tully! The answer is no!' screamed Barbu. 'Barbu D'Anvers! The evilest, foulest, baddest genius that this island has ever seen! To conclude, me!' Tully rubbed the bump that was popping up above his left ear. 'Sometimes,' Barbu sighed, throwing himself on a purple chaise longue and lifting a hand to his forehead, 'it's a terrible burden being quite so very brilliant. In fact, it's exhausting.'

'Can I get you a small drink, Mr Barbu?' asked Tully, wondering if that's what he should do in the circumstances.

'A small drink?' spat Barbu, sitting bolt upright. 'A SMALL drink? Are you saying I'm short?'

'No, Mr Barbu.' The stupid sidekick gulped. 'You? Short? Ha ha ha ha ha! As if!'

'Hmmm,' said Barbu, through narrowed eyes, 'that's all right then. Now read back the evil plan that I have dictated.'

Tully stuck his corn-cob cigar in the side of his mouth and took out a battered notepad. Clearing his throat a little, he began to read.

My Brilliant Evil Plan
by Mr Barbu D'Anvers.

1. Find out who stole the Katzin Stone.
2. Kill them.
3. Steal it.
4. Sell it and buy Cooper Island with the proceeds.
5. Rename Cooper Island Barbu D'Anvers I land and make everyone my slave.
6. Buy some shoes with special hidden heels.

'I don't want them for medicinal reasons,' snarled Barbu, shooting Tully a glare. 'I just like them. Because they are fashionable.'

'Yes, Mr Barbu,' said Tully, feeling a little uncomfortable. 'That's the end of the brilliant evil plan.'

Barbu was motivated by one thing: greed. In all his years as a devoted member of the Criminal Element fraternity, Barbu had made it his mission to accumulate as much wealth as he could so that one day he could achieve his ultimate goal – to purchase and control the whole of Cooper Island. How he had managed to evade capture and remain at large might shock the more law-abiding of you, but Barbu was so sneaky and devious that he was always able to pin the blame on a lesser criminal than himself and skip away as free as a bird. For Theodore P. Goodman and the rest of the good citizens of Cooper, this was intensely annoying. But there it was. Barbu was the thorn in Cooper's side. And he had no intention of stopping.

'Oh!' cried Barbu, leaping off the chaise longue. 'I haven't been this excited since I embezzled the Cooper Frail-Old-Lady Fund! I stole all that money! Right from under Theodore P. Goodman's stupid nose! And there was nothing he could do about it! I am so very brilliant and so very evil! Bask in my glory, Tully. Go on. Bask in it!'

'Yes, sir,' said Tully, walking forward until he was towering over his tiny master.

'No, that's too close,' said Barbu, staring up the nostrils of Tully's broken nose. 'Bask a little further off. So, Tully,' declared Barbu, as the henchman took a few steps back, 'we must turn our minds to item Number One on the Brilliant Evil Plan agenda. Namely – find out who stole the Katzin Stone.' He closed his eyes and thought for a long moment.

Tully stood quietly by, wondering if he was still meant to be basking. 'Interesting!' declared Barbu, opening his eyes again. 'I have developed a theorem and also a stratagem. Quickly! To the drawingboard!' Barbu scampered across the room to a large black drawingboard. Taking up a piece of chalk, he began to write.

> **A man discovers the greatest jewel ever found. The
> man is killed. Why is the man killed? To get him
> out of the way. It's standard evil procedure. But
> who is this killer? It wasn't me.**

Barbu underlined his point with a flourish. 'I can therefore, and with some authority, eliminate myself from the list of suspects. Cross me off the list Tully.'

Tully turned to a blank page of his notepad and made an elaborate scribble.

'But the question is,' added Barbu, pacing and thinking, 'what did the killer-thief do next? Pass me yesterday's edition of the *Early Worm*, will you?' Tully picked up the island's most popular morning newspaper and handed it to his master. '"Furore as Fabulous New Fish Freezer Opened on Farside Miles from the

Docks" – no, that's not it. "Cooper's Corn Crumble Grumble Causes Rumbles" – it's not that either . . . Ah, here it is, "Katzin Stone Stealing Scandal" . . . blah blah blah . . . "Museum authorities have brought in Cooper's greatest living detective Theodore P. Goodman . . ." my old nemesis, makes things spicy, never mind that – he's still the most boring man I know . . . "Investigations into the theft have revealed that all is not as it seemed. A source close to the detective said, 'Somehow, someone replaced the real Katzin Stone with a fake that melted on the way to the museum. My dog helped me find a bit of it. But I almost died. It was brilliant. . .'" Interesting . . . fetch me the *D.I.C.E.*, will you, Tully? I want to check out some of our forger friends.'

The *D.I.C.E.*, of course, was the *Directory of the Island's Criminal Elements*, a sort of bad version of the telephone book, where anyone employed in skulduggery and wrongdoing was listed. Sadly it was quite a large book. Tully dropped it on the table with a thump.

'Now then,' said Barbu D'Anvers, picking up the blood-red book and flicking through it. 'F for Forgers. Let's have a look. F, F, F! False Document Makers . . . Fernickety Safe Pickers . . . Forgers! Now then, let's see – Faked Fingers and Toes, Faked Implants – we can make your legs bigger by . . . goodness. That much? Hmmm. I'll just make a note of that number. Not for myself, you understand. I've got a . . . friend. Tiny legs. *I'm* not short.'

Tully stared dead ahead and said nothing.

'Faked Fruit, Faked Organisms, Faked Stones! Aha!' cried Barbu, tapping at the page in triumph. 'We have it, Tully. Now then, let's see who's listed . . . Harwood Birch? Oh dear, no, this *D.I.C.E.* isn't quite up to date.'

'How do you know, Mr Barbu?' asked Tully, looking puzzled.

'Because I killed Harwood Birch six months ago. Covered him in jam and dropped him into a hornet's nest.'

'Oooh, that's not nice,' said Tully, sucking in his breath.

'No,' agreed Barbu, 'I suppose it's what you would call a sticky end. Ha ha ha ha! Do you get it? Sticky end?' But Tully didn't get it, because your standard henchman doesn't possess the DNA strand that gives people a sense of humour so he just stood very still and hoped that his tiny master wouldn't notice.

'Who's next? Visser Haanstra. Hmmm. I remember him. Used him on a job about five years ago. Looks promising. We must get on to this, Tully. At once. Do you understand?' shouted Barbu, throwing the *D.I.C.E.* at him for good measure.

Tully nodded and rubbed his head for the second time that day. Sometimes being an evil sidekick was a very thankless task.

CHAPTER 12

Mrs Speckle had run out of corn crumbles. If Mrs Speckle had been an Emergency Coordination Officer at a press conference she would have put a picture of an empty plate on an overhead projector, pointed at it with a stick and described the situation as 'critical'. But she wasn't. All the same, the fact she had run out of Theodore P. Goodman's favourite biscuits with moments to go before his morning pot of peppermint-tea was like dis-covering you're half way up Everest without socks on.

Mrs Speckle looked at her knitted watch. By her reckoning she had fifteen minutes and thirty-four seconds before peppermint tea time. It was going to be tight. To make matters worse, Mr Hankley, the island's finest maker of cakes and sweet treats, was attending a conference on puff pastry so the bakery was closed. Reluctantly, Mrs Speckle accepted that if her employer was to have his biscuits then there was only one thing to be done.

*

Wilma had not slept well. The mattress she and Pickle were forced to curl up on was immediately below a large and rusty pipe that had gurgled and moaned all night. In any case, Wilma was too excited to sleep. The events of the previous day were so overwhelming she had spent the night buzzing with ideas about stolen stones, suspects and sugar. Somehow she had to become Theodore P. Goodman's apprentice.

Mrs Waldock had ordered liver-porridge-potato cakes for her mid-morning snack, and as Wilma stood on a stool stirring gristly lumps of liver into bubbling oats and crushed potatoes she came up with an idea. 'Perhaps,' she said, turning to look at Pickle, who was staring up at the saucepan and dribbling, 'if I could solve this Katzin case mostly on my own, perhaps Mr Goodman would quite like me to be his apprentice? What do you think about that? Then one day he can help me to deduction my very own family history . . .'

Pickle said nothing. He was too fascinated by the large lump of liver dangling dangerously from the end of Wilma's wooden spoon, but sadly, just as it was about to drip to the floor, the front-door knocker rapped three times. Wilma dropped the spoon back into the saucepan and jumped down to answer it.

'Hmph,' said Mrs Speckle, fidgeting in her knitted wellingtons as Wilma appeared. 'Yes, well. The thing is I've run out of

corn crumbles. And it's Mr Goodman's eleven o clock tea. And I wondered if Mrs Waldock has —'

'Got some to spare?' butted in Wilma, sensing an opportunity. 'I'll have to check her biscuit barrel. And then I'll bring them over. Won't be long.' And with that she slammed the door in Mrs Speckle's face.

'Quick, Pickle,' said Wilma, running back to the kitchen and tipping the sloppy liver-porridge-potato cakes into a bowl. 'Take this to Mrs Waldock and I'll find the corn crumbles.'

Putting the rim of the bowl in Pickle's mouth, Wilma turned on her heels and ran to Mrs Waldock's pantry. It was a small, dusty room with floor-to-ceiling shelves on every wall. The higher ones were filled with large jars of pickled tongues and pig's trotters in syrup that had sat for so long they were almost black with grime. Lower down there were tins of sheep's eyes and bird claws, bags of dried grasshoppers and boxes of ants dipped in chocolate. In the far corner of the pantry there was a large, wooden barrel with the word 'Biskits' carved into its exterior. Wilma pushed the heavy lid aside and peered in. At first, she thought it was empty, but pushing back the lid a little further she could see that right down at the bottom there was one corn crumble left.

*

Mrs Speckle was standing looking at her tea tray. The teapot was steaming, but the empty plate was staring back at her. This was a bad business. She looked again at her knitted watch. Three seconds to peppermint-tea time, two, one just as the second hand hit the teapot on her watch face, in walked Theodore P. Goodman. 'Hello, Mrs Speckle,' said the detective, marching through the kitchen. 'I'll take tea in my study, thank you.'

'Right away, Mr Goodman,' said Mrs Speckle, picking up the tray. 'The thing is —'

'And so will I,' said Wilma, waltzing through after him.

'Hold it right there, young lady!' said Mrs Speckle, startled.

Wilma turned and held up the corn crumble. 'It's fine, Mrs Speckle. I come with a biscuit. Thank you.'

'Corn crumble?' asked Theodore, moustache twitching. 'Although I'm sure Mrs Speckle has plenty. All the same, a corn crumble is a corn crumble.'

'Never go detecting on an empty stomach, eh, Mr Goodman?' Wilma trilled. 'Top tip number ten, Mrs Speckle,' she added.

'Well, I never,' said Mrs Speckle giving a little huff to register her disapproval. But Wilma had got her out of a potentially awkward biscuit-based disaster and for that, reluctantly, she was grateful.

*

Walking into Theodore P. Goodman's study was like Christmas squared. There were too many things for Wilma to look at and she was so overexcited that all she could do was twirl on the spot to take it all in. 'Ooooh,' she said, coming to a sudden stop. 'That made me feel a bit sick. Like when Michael Lamb – he was at the Institute and smelled of sprouts – spun me round by my arms when I was six. I threw up on his foot.'

'Very nice, I'm sure,' said Mrs Speckle, frowning as she watched the corn crumble in Wilma's hand. 'I'll just take that biscuit, shall I?' she added, giving the girl a stern look.

But Wilma was far too distracted to notice and bounced over to a wall with diagrams, pictures and pins all over it. 'What's this?' she asked, waving the precious corn crumble in its direction.

'That,' said the detective, standing up and reaching for the biscuit, 'is my Clue Board. Crimes are like puzzles. Each clue, on its own, might reveal the answer, but a lot of clues can help you piece the problem together. So this Clue Board helps when it comes to mysteries so deep they're quite hard to fathom.'

'What's fathom?' asked Wilma, jumping on to a chair just before the world-famous detective could reach the biscuit.

'Well,' began Theodore, moustache twitching, 'it can be a nautical term by which current depth is determined. But in this context, to fathom something means to understand it. So if you

102

were unable to fathom the evidence you're looking at now, then that would mean you were unable to work it out.'

'You're always using words that mean two things at once,' said Wilma. 'That's tricky.' Wilma examined the Clue Board as she spoke. It was covered in handwritten notes at the centre of which was a small blueprint of the vault where the Katzin Stone had been kept. To its right there was a picture of the stone itself, and from that two long pieces of string, one of which led to a picture of Alan Katzin and his aunt enjoying a lemon meringue pie in happier days while the other led to a second picture of the empty plinth at the museum. Along the bottom of the board there was a stencilled heading that read 'Suspects', under which there was a mugshot of Jeremy Burling and next to him the word 'Magician?' Finally, to the left of the board there was a section marked 'Method', in which there was a receipt from someone called Penbert for 'One sugary-looking shard'. You always write things down, don't you, Mr Goodman? That's top tip number six,' said Wilma, staring upwards. She thought long and hard about everything she'd seen and, as she lost herself in a trail of deductions, she inadvertently took a large bite out of the corn crumble in her hand.

'Ohhhh!' puffed Mrs Speckle, who threw her arms as far into the air as her double-knitted cardigan would allow. 'Well, that's that!' she mumbled as she left the room. 'Lowsiders and biscuits. Never in all my days!'

Theodore frowned, gave a small sigh and returned to his desk. 'Yes, well. Anyway, I should be getting on. The missing Katzin Stone and all that.'

Wilma, whose mouth was full of biscuit, turned and held up a finger. 'I have been doing some contemplating and I think I have a deduction,' she announced, spitting corn-crumble crumbs everywhere. 'When I saw the bit of the fake Katzin Stone, I thought it looked like caramel, but I told you that already. So I think the fake Katzin Stone must have been made by someone who's brilliant at toffee shapes. But not just toffee shapes, because it was clever the way it all melted but deadly because it turned into poison. It's a bit confusing, because anyone who loved making toffee would never love making poison as well.'

'Hmmm,' pondered Theodore. 'That's not quite how it works but . . . good try . . .'

Wilma grinned delightedly. 'Does this mean I'm your apprentice now?' she asked, swallowing the last bit of biscuit.

Theodore stopped what he was doing and looked at her but before he could answer there was a knock at the study door. It was Mrs Speckle.

'Sorry to interrupt, Mr Goodman. Telegram's just come. It's from Inspector Lemone.'

'Ah, excellent,' said Theodore, holding his hand out. 'Thank you, Mrs Speckle.' He flipped over the sealed end of the telegram and read it out loud:

```
Meet me at the lab. Dr Kooks has news.
```

'Who's Dr Kooks, Mr Goodman?' asked Wilma.

'Titus Kooks. He conducts forensic tests on dead bodies.'

'Forensic?' asked Wilma.

Theodore P. Goodman, who was a very serious and thorough detective, gave an impatient sigh. Here he was, in the middle of a deadly investigation and this small, inquisitive child was taking up his valuable time and eating his biscuits. All the same, he never liked to be rude and spotting something on his shelf, he realized how he could extricate himself from this inconvenient situation.

'Here,' said the detective, handing Wilma the small dictionary he had pulled off his shelf. 'You can keep that to look up any words you don't understand.'

'Can I come?' asked Wilma, following him out of the study.

'No,' said Theodore, striding away. 'You're too young to see a dead body.' And with that, he swept out of the house.

As Wilma wandered back into Mrs Waldock's kitchen she stared at the dictionary in her hand and flipped to forensic. 'Science

used in a court of law' she read. 'Hmmm. I suspect there'll be more clues. Sounds too important to miss. And I ought to start putting those top tips into practice so I can impress Mr Goodman even more . . .'

'Wilma!' shouted her employer from the adjacent room. 'Where are my liver-porridge-potato cakes?'

Wilma gasped and looked down at Pickle, who was lying on his back, legs in the air and snoring, next to a very empty bowl. It would appear that Wilma hadn't been the only one to eat something they shouldn't.

CHAPTER 13

Visser Haanstra was tired. Leaning back on his heels, he held the base of his back with his hands and rubbed. He wore a scruffy cloth cap on his head and had spectacles shaped like kidney beans. 'I've run out of glue,' said a small voice. It was Janty, Visser's ten-year-old son. Pushing a mass of unruly dark curls out of his eyes, the boy bent forward on to his father's workbench and rested his chin into his hands. His eyes were a soft, watery grey and his nose was freckled. He wore a dark green jumper, full of holes and frayed at the arms, his brown shorts were covered in small black patches and the plimsolls on his feet were scuffed and torn. His hands were stained, his nails dirty. All in all he gave off a rather grubby aspect, as if he'd been scraped up from the bottom of a bin.

Visser took off his spectacles and wiped at his eyes with his handkerchief.

'I think there's some in the outhouse. You can look there. Show me what you're making.'

Janty held up a half-finished brooch. Visser took it in his hands and peered at it. 'What's it supposed to be?'

'A squirrel, but I haven't started the tail yet so it looks more like a peanut.'

'Not bad, Janty,' said Visser. 'We'll make a forger of you yet.'

The more well-behaved of you might be shocked that a father involved in illegal enterprises would encourage a son to do the same. But a family business is a family business and because Janty was an only child, the responsibility to carry on the tradition of being bad fell to him. If he'd had a pesky brother or a very naughty sister then Janty might have been able to be an acrobat or an insurance salesman, but he didn't, so that was that.

Visser's workshop was situated in a basement on the edge of the small rundown village of Much Mithering on the Lowside of the island. It was a clutter of tools, books and bags of coloured sugar. In the corner was a large iron stove on top of which sat a bubbling pot. Next to the pot was a heated flat stone covered with spatulas and tongs, and next to that was a steaming cupboard where thin sheets of warm caramel hung on racks. The air was heavy with a sickly sweet smell, and a warm mist filled the room. Visser unscrewed the vice on his workbench. 'Janty,' he said, holding out a small delicate item, 'take this. It's the copy of the LeGassick casket.'

The entire thing was made from sugar. 'It's wonderful, Father,' said Janty, eyes wide with admiration as he looked from the replica to the newspaper cutting showing the original. 'Will I be ever able to make something like that?'

'One day,' said Visser, patting his son on the back. 'One day. Now, wrap it up for me in a packing box. Then bring me the order book.'

'Yes, Father,' said the young boy, jumping down from the workbench stool.

With his work done for the day, Visser undid his leather apron and hung it on a hook. Reaching into a cupboard next to the stove, he lifted down a sturdy black soup pan and filled it with barley, meadow grass and reed juice. Then, unclipping the lid of a seeping yellow container, he took a handful of squirming slugs and threw them into the brew. As he stirred, Visser heard the door behind him click. 'Make sure you've washed your hands,' said the forger, lifting the spoon to his mouth to give it a lick.

'I don't think there'll be any need for that,' said a voice, and suddenly Visser felt an iron grip around his throat. Choking, he fell against the soup pan, sending it spilling across the floor. Visser clawed at the fingers around his neck, but it was

hopeless. He was being dragged backwards, away from the stove, and in one quick movement he found himself twisted about and staring at a very short and very well-dressed man. 'Hello, Visser,' said the voice, holding out his silver-topped walking cane and giving the forger a prod. 'Remember me? That'll do for now, Tully. Let him go.'

The henchman released his hold on Visser's neck and the forger fell to the floor, coughing and spluttering. 'Slug stew?' said Barbu, flicking one of the spilt creatures from his boot. 'How very rustic.'

'What do you want, Barbu?' coughed Visser, as he scrabbled back against the leg of his workbench. He had to warn Janty. Under the rim of the marble top there was a silent alarm. If he could just reach up and press it . . . SLAM! Down came the silver-topped cane, smashing Visser's fingers against the leg of the bench. 'Aaaaaagh!' cried out the forger.

'You wouldn't be trying to tell someone that we're here, would you, Mr Haanstra?' said Barbu, poking his cane under Visser's chin and pushing upwards. 'Tully, check that we're alone.'

'Yes, Mr Barbu,' said the henchman, walking in the direction of the door.

'There's no one else here!' yelled Visser, clutching his broken fingers with a grimace.

'I'll be the judge of that,' said Barbu, with an evil sneer. 'Boo hoo, Mr Haanstra, have I hurt you? I'd hate to have to hurt you again. But I'm a man who likes to know things. And when anyone knows something that I don't that makes me very, very angry. What can I say? I'm a nightmare.'

Barbu D'Anvers lowered himself into the workshop armchair as Visser stared wild-eyed at the door leading in from the outhouse. 'So, Mr Haanstra, let's get down to it,' began Barbu. 'The Katzin Stone – where is it?'

'What?' said Visser, shaking. 'How should I know?'

Barbu tapped at the top of his cane and tilted his head to one side. 'Let me put that a different way. You tell me where the Katzin Stone is and I might not break the fingers in your other hand.'

'I-I don't know what you're talking about,' stammered Visser.

The back door burst open. 'No one there, Mr Barbu,' declared Tully with a shrug.

Visser's chest heaved with relief. Janty must have heard all the noise and realized it meant trouble. He would have followed procedure and hidden himself in a hollow tree at the bottom of the garden.

'Good,' said Barbu . . .

*

It's at this point that gentle eyes should turn away. We don't need to know all the gory, horrible details of what Barbu did next. So let's think about something more uplifting, like finding a forgotten fruity chewy sweet in the bottom of a pocket or discovering a kitten in a sock. We don't need to know that Barbu crushed Visser's glasses between Tully's buttocks. We don't need to know that he stuffed mashed carrot up his nose. And we certainly don't need to know that Tully tied him up, hoisted him over the iron stove and lowered his feet into the bubbling pot of boiling sugar.

'Cut him down, Tully,' snarled Barbu ten minutes later, twirling his cane with menace. Tully produced a large cutlass from inside his overcoat and swiped at the rope. As it sliced in two, Visser slumped to the floor. He was bleeding and broken.

'Now then,' whispered Barbu, bending down to the forger's face, 'tell me what I want to know.'

Visser coughed weakly. 'The Katzin Stone,' he began, 'is . . . '

But at that exact moment a dart struck him in the neck. The forger looked startled, went stiff and passed out.

'What the . . . ?!' screamed Barbu, twisting about to see where the dart had come from. An air vent up in the wall snapped shut. 'Tully! The air vent! Quickly!'

Tully scrabbled to his feet and ran to where the dart had

come from but it was too late. 'There's no one there, boss,' he said, peering up into the tiny opening.

'No! No! Nooooo!' screamed Barbu, striking his cane down hard on the workbench. 'No one out-evils me!'

'It goes a long way back,' said Tully. 'It could lead anywhere.'

Barbu pulled the dart from the unconcious forger's neck. 'Poisoned!' he declared. 'Things have taken a twist, Tully. Someone has foiled Barbu D'Anvers.' Throwing the dart to the floor, Barbu raised his face to the ceiling and screamed. 'I'm FURIOUS! And I will kill whoever blew that dart. Come on – there's only one place to go to find out who it was.'

'Up the air vent?' asked Tully, scratching his head. 'I think I'm a bit big —'

'No! Not up the air vent!' screamed Barbu, bashing his sidekick over the head with his cane. 'To the place where all the island's lowlives and rotten tittle-tattles gather on the Lowside: the Twelve Rats' Tails. Still, we have had a very long day. And it is exhausting torturing people. So we'll go there tomorrow. My cloak, Tully.'

And as the stupid henchman draped his master's cloak over his shoulders, off they swept.

A dread silence fell in the workshop. Visser's body lay lifeless at the foot of the stove. A slug crawled out from the dark and

slithered over his broken hand and then, from the gloom of the doorway, a small snivelling pierced the quiet. It was Janty. Certain that whoever had been there was gone, he had crept back to the workshop. Horrified by what he now saw, he took his father's body in his arms. As his tears fell on his father's face, he felt a small breath on his cheek. Visser was still alive! 'Father!' cried Janty.

'Listen to me,' whispered Visser, mustering his last scraps of strength. 'The order book . . . you must hide it. Keep it safe. And trust no one. Leave here and don't come back.'

'But, Father . . .'

'Do as I say!' urged Visser, fighting back the pain. 'Tell no one! Never forget the forger's code, Janty! We never reveal our clients. Ever! You must carry on . . . you have the gift . . . promise me . . . you will be a great forger . . . a great . . .' And then, with one, long look that held the promise of all of Janty's years, Visser's soul passed into the dark.

'Father!' screamed Janty, shaking his head. 'Father!

Another character dead? A poor boy orphaned? And we're not even halfway through. Oh, this is just awful.

114

CHAPTER 14

Titus Kooks wished he was an opera singer. Holding a dissected liver in one hand and a pot of brains in the other he stood, eyes closed, and sung his lungs out. Penbert, his efficient assistant, who hated opera music, especially when Titus sang it, stood with her fingers in her ears and waited for it to stop. The song Titus was currently singing was a particularly bad one because Titus had written it himself. The song was called *I Feel Offal*, which will serve as a small clue as to quite how bad it was. Luckily for Penbert, who had better things to do, like getting on with her matchstick model of a chicken, the song was almost at its end.

'And though I am quite keeeeeeeen!' sang Titus, arms aloft. 'To extract your spleeeeeeeeeeen! There is nothing badder! Than a mouldy bladddddddddddder!' As the last note rang out, Titus slumped forward into a dramatic bow.

Penbert took her fingers out of her ears. 'Bravo, Dr Kooks,' she said, adding a small, half-hearted smatter of applause. 'Now, as I was saying, I'm not sure if hydrofluoric acid is going to work because . . .'

'Was it rich?' asked Dr Kooks, looking up. 'My voice – did it have timbre? Did it resonate?'

Penbert blinked and pushed her incredibly thick spectacles to the top of her nose. 'I think,' she began, shuffling her feet, 'that it may have been better than yesterday.'

Dr Kooks thumped the pot of brains down on to a work surface. 'Then I am improving. Here, take these. Analyse them for confusion and befuddlement. Let me have your report by the end of the day.'

The lab, where all Cooper Island criminal scientific investigations were conducted, was a clutter of test tubes, microscopes and dissected body parts in jars. On the wall were two thin vertical blackboards, each stencilled with the white outlines of a body which, in turn, were covered with chalked arrows and scribbles, the largest of which read 'Unnaturally smelly feet' followed by a long line of exclamation marks. In the corner of the room was a fume cupboard for the examination of toxic chemicals, a bookshelf rammed to bursting with books, files and papers and a series of hooks on the wall with masks, aprons and gloves hanging from them. In the centre of the room there was

a large metal table for the examination of dead bodies and to the left two small desks, one heaving with documents, opera magazines and random beakers of half-drunk tea, the other very neat and tidy with a small, unfinished matchstick chicken on it.

Penbert, who was always known by her last name, took her job extremely seriously. Dr Kooks, on the other hand, did not and he liked nothing better than to play small practical jokes on his assistant, like the time he put a severed foot in her operating clogs. Penbert, because she was only the assistant and was determined to be serious, bore all of Dr Kook's nonsense with an air of stoic tolerance.

One of Penbert's favourite serious jobs at the lab was providing visitors with official passes and so, when Theodore P. Goodman, the world-famous detective, and Inspector Lemone, Cooper Island's only police officer, arrived at ten past four, she took a small but significant delight in logging them into the Visitor's Book and handing them large Visitor Badges to pin on to their lapels. 'Thank you, Penbert,' said Theodore as he put his badge on, before adding, 'You've pinned yours upside down, Inspector.' An oversight that had not gone unnoticed by Penbert.

'Now then,' began Theodore, shaking Dr Kooks firmly by the hand, 'the shard from the fake Katzin Stone. Have you managed to examine it?'

'Certainly have, Goodman,' boomed Titus, rubbing his belly. 'You were right. It was made of sugar.'

'A special sort of sugar,' added Penbert, reaching for her clipboard.

'Yes,' said Titus, throwing an arm in Penbert's direction, 'special sort. Hmmm. What was it again, Penbert?'

'It's a sugar called Ambeedextrose,' said Penbert, reading from her notes.

'Interesting,' said Theodore, fingering his magnifying glass.

'So the thief is a sugar expert?' said the Inspector, licking the end of his pencil and making a note.

'Not necessarily, Inspector,' interjected Theodore. 'Let's not jump to conclusions.'

'Nice sugar, is it?' asked the Inspector, eyebrows rising a little. 'Make cakes with it? Biscuits? Meringues?'

'It's not that sort of sugar,' said Penbert, shaking her head. 'It has a very interesting molecular structure. It's thicker than normal. We also found a trace of poison on it. That was unusual too. Comes from the bark of the very rare Cynta tree. I suspect its presence is incidental. May have been transferred by touch.'

'That would explain the smell on the shard,' said Theodore, reaching for his battered leather notebook. 'So the presence of the poison was probably unintentional. Fascinating.'

'Yes,' nodded Dr Kooks, wafting a dismissive hand. 'And

it had some writing on it, a sort of inscription. What was it again, Penbert?'

'It said, "I Made It", Dr Kooks,' said Penbert, consulting her clipboard, 'and was in a very unusual font, of which I've taken some super-magnified resonant images . . .'

Just as Penbert was about to unclip her pictures there was a loud rap at the door. Penbert glanced up at the clock and frowned. She wasn't expecting other visitors and, in any event, wasn't sure she had more than two visitor badges. This was a worrying development. 'Excuse me,' she said, putting down her clipboard.

Standing at the door was what appeared to be a very short man with a ginger beard so massive it covered three-quarters of his face. He was also wearing a large floppy hat, dark glasses and patchwork overalls that were at least ten sizes too big. By his feet was a lumpy hessian bag that for some reason was moving of its own accord. 'I have come,' said the man in a strangely high voice, 'to fix the plumbing.'

Penbert gave a short frown. 'But there's not a problem with the plumbing,' she said. 'And besides, we already have our quota of visitors for today. Only two at a time. Thank you.' Penbert smiled quietly to herself. That would deal with the lack of badges problem.

'No,' said the man, inching forward and straining to see into

119

the lab. 'Definitely a problem. I've been sent by the . . . um . . . the . . . Central Plumbing Bureau.'

'The Central Plumbing Bureau?' asked Penbert, eyes narrowing.

'Yes,' said the man, with a nod. 'They deal with plumbing. Mostly.'

Penbert gave the man an even longer frown. 'Are you really a plumber?' she said, folding her arms and pursing her lips.

'Oh yes!' blustered the man, hat falling down over his dark glasses. 'I know lots about plumbing. Like that there . . . that's a sink! Look at it, over there! Just past that detective!'

'How do you know I'm a detective?' asked Theodore, who had been watching from the lab. 'Bring that man in, Penbert. Something's not quite right here.'

'But we've only got two Visitor's Badges,' said Penbert, feeling a little anxious.

'Never mind that now!' boomed Dr Kooks, who had marched over to the door to stare at the suspect plumber. 'In you come, young man! Let's get the measure of you!'

The man bent down to pick up his bag, which was now wriggling so intensely he had to grab it with both arms. He staggered into the lab, where everyone stood and stared as he tripped over one leg of his overalls, got his foot caught in the hem of the other and fell head first into a pile of neatly stacked files. The plumber's bag, sliding halfway across the floor, sud-

denly ripped open and out of it, to everyone's surprise, stepped a beagle wearing a pair of goggles and a cap. Not only that, but he also appeared to have a very thick ginger moustache and a tool belt tied around his waist. Theodore snatched up the young man by the neck of his overalls and with one deft tug removed his beard. 'As I suspected,' said the great detective as he looked down at Wilma. 'Now this won't do. It won't do at all.'

'The thing is,' began Wilma as she stared back up at the detective, 'it's very important that I practise gathering clues. You know, for contemplating and deductions. And crimes are like puzzles. Like you said. So I just thought I ought to come. In a disguise from Mrs Waldock's trunk. Because sometimes they can be cunning. According to your top tip number seven. So I thought that it would probably be best . . .' Wilma trailed off – the great detective didn't exactly look impressed.

Theodore P. Goodman, who was a very important and very serious man, gave a little sigh. 'Wilma,' he explained, handing the young orphan her large hairy beard, 'you work for Mrs Waldock. Now what will she say when she finds out you're running around chasing clues when I suspect you should be doing your chores? Still, you're here now. So stand over there with the Inspector and try not to trip over anything else.'

'But I've got no more Visitor Badges!' protested Penbert,

who was even more agitated now that her carefully alphabetized files were scattered all over the lab floor.

'Here you are, Wilma,' said the Inspector, handing her his Visitor Badge. 'You have mine. I'll just stand here on police business. Don't need a visitor badge for that.'

'Actually, you do,' muttered Penbert, with a tut. 'And —'

'Penbert,' interrupted Dr Kooks, rolling his eyes, 'do be quiet. Now then, Mr Goodman. The inscription on the shard. Here's the picture. Look at that. "I Made It". What do you think of that?'

'Hmmm,' said Theodore, using his magnifying glass to take a closer look. 'It should be "I Made This". Masterful forgery using sugar and sloppy grammar? It can only be one man – Visser Haanstra. Remember him, Inspector?'

'Ummm . . . on the tip of my tongue, Goodman . . . wait . . . hang on . . . no. No, I don't,' said the Inspector, tapping his pencil on the end of his nose.

'Case of the Silver Mask, Mr Goodman!' blurted Wilma. 'The one where Barbu D'Anvers set a trap using crabs. I've got it on my Clue Ring!' She excitedly waved her collection of cuttings at the detective.

'That's the one, Wilma!' declared Theodore. 'We need to see him first thing tomorrow,' he went on, with purpose. 'Visser is a masterly craftsman but I'll wager this wasn't his idea.'

'What about Jeremy Burling?' asked Wilma. 'Because he's a suspicious.'

'A suspect, not a suspicious. There's a difference. No. I spoke with him this morning. I think he *believes* he saw Alan on the morning of his murder – and Captain Brock can attest to a visitor who answered to that name – but, well, disguises are cunning, Wilma. Jeremy's not our man. But I'll bet that mysterious visitor is, or my name's not Theodore P. Goodman. We must move fast, Inspector. Before the net tightens. Now then, Titus, what of Alan Katzin and his aunt? How were they killed?'

Dr Kooks's face fell and an air of seriousness descended. 'Strangest thing, Goodman,' he said, with a small shake of his head. 'Strangest thing. We found virtually nothing. No wounds, no bruises, no poisons in the blood, nothing. We did find one small fish scale on Alan Katzin's aunt. But she was a keen cook by all accounts so that might explain that. And they were each holding a sprig of lavender.'

'But if there were no wounds, no poisonous substances . . . what killed them?' the Inspector asked, scratching his head.

'We're totally unable to establish how or why,' said Penbert. 'But there was one thing . . .' She stopped mid-sentence and glanced at Doctor Kooks.

'Well, out with it,' urged Theodore, stroking his moustache.

'The thing is,' said Dr Kooks, his voice falling to a whisper, 'their hearts were frozen. Frozen solid.'

Wilma felt her mouth drop open. Pickle yelped and shook his tool belt. Things had taken a spooky turn.

CHAPTER 15

Everyone knows that there are some places that people not wishing to get into trouble should probably never go, and on Cooper Island that place was the Twelve Rats' Tails, a notorious hangout for Criminal Elements. The tavern was tucked into a dark corner of Rotten-Egg Alley, a stinking, sewage-strewn street on the west side of the Cooper Island docks. A creaking wooden sign hung above its mangy door. On it was a faded painting of twelve severed rats' tails and beneath it a dire warning: 'No one Welkom' it read. 'Go awaye'.

The walls of the Twelve Rats' Tails oozed with dirt and sweat, and the room was filled with clouds of pipe smoke and the smell of stale beer. The tavern was a maze of nooks and corners that even in the early morning were dark and packed with hunched thugs and lowlives, caps pulled down low over foreheads and heavy jackets that hid a multitude of sins. As Barbu D'Anvers

entered, he took a quick glance around him and curled his lip
into a trademark sneer. 'Utterly disgusting,' he snarled, lifting his
cape to his nose. 'I'd forgotten. Don't let me take my gloves off,
Tully. Well, what are you standing there for? Go and find him!'

As Tully slunk off into the fog of pipe smoke Barbu noticed
that a grizzled woman in a broken top hat was staring at him.
She had a patch over one eye and was sucking on what appeared
to be a long, thin bone. 'Revolting,' muttered Barbu under his
breath. Sitting next to her was another woman whose face he
couldn't quite see. She was wearing a heavy shawl that was pulled
up over the top of her head so that, in the dank of the room, all
Barbu could make out of her face were two tiny pinpricks of
light as the candle on their table picked out her eyes and one
long, dark curl hanging down her cheek. She was playing with
a deck of cards, splitting the pack and shuffling with great skill,
her red fingernails flashing in the candlelight. Whoever she was,
she seemed very interested in Barbu, but then, as Barbu thought
to himself, he was the island's most notorious criminal. 'Probably wants my autograph,' he muttered with a shrug.

'Over here, Mr Barbu,' said a voice cutting through the
gloom. It was Tully and he was gesturing towards a particularly
pitch-black corner. As Barbu sat down, the man he had come to
see took a large swig from the tankard in front of him and ran
a filthy hand across his mouth. Flatnose Detoit had the sort of

face that looked as if it wasn't quite on right. Everything about him was skewed and off centre, his eyes sloped down to the left, his mouth veered off to the right while his nose, so squashed as to be almost imperceptible, seemed not to know which way it was going.

'You know why I'm here, Flatnose,' began Barbu, placing his cane on the table. 'The Katzin Stone. Who stole it? Where can I find them? How many people do I need to hurt?'

Flatnose shook his head slowly and leaned forward. 'Here's the thing, Mr D'Anvers,' he whispered, nose rattling as he spoke, 'no one knows. Not a peep from anyone. Not since this . . .' Flatnose reached into his pocket and pulled out a crushed newspaper. 'Look at that,' he added, tapping at that morning's headline. 'Hearts frozen solid, Mr D'Anvers. No normal man can do that.'

Barbu's eyes narrowed. 'So? So someone can freeze people's hearts. Boring! What's wrong with using a gun? Or a pointy stick? Whoever it is, he's clearly just showing off. Which I'm forced to admire him for. That aside, I'm still going to kill him and get that stone. So, Flatnose, I just want to know who it is.' Barbu picked up his cane and shoved it into the informant's chest. 'And I want to know now.'

'But I don't know, Mr D'Anvers, I swear it,' said Flatnose, wild-eyed. 'Everyone's been talking about Visser Haanstra

being killed. Great forger. Terrible loss to the Criminal Element fraternity. He knew who did it. But the secret died with him. Although . . .' the snitch added, in a low whisper, 'they do say he had an order book. Kept all his secrets in it. If you can find that, then you might have the name you want.'

'Order book?' snapped Barbu, twisting the cane harder into Flatnose's chest. 'What order book?'

'Visser kept an order book,' coughed Flatnose, gasping. 'Never let anyone see it. Apart from his son, Janty. Now he's the only person left alive who knows what it looks like and where it is.'

Barbu released his cane. 'So Visser has a son . . .' he mused. 'Hmmm. Interesting.'

'Probably quite small,' said Tully, thinking aloud. 'Easy to kill.'

'There's nothing wrong with small, Tully,' barked Barbu, rapping the henchman on the forehead with the end of his cane. 'No. We shan't kill this boy . . . yet. I have a feeling he might be of use. Pay Flatnose, Tully. And meet me outside.'

The early-morning air was cold and piercing as Barbu swept out of the Twelve Rats' Tails and as he stood in the alleyway he was aware of a presence to his left. Turning on his heel, he held out his cane. 'You there,' he shouted, 'come forward!'

Out from the murk stepped the shawl-clad woman who had been playing with the cards. She was hunched over a stick

128

and carrying a basket. In her hand she was holding something small and blue. 'Lucky lavender, mister,' she mumbled, creeping closer and holding the flower aloft.

'Get away!' shouted Barbu, swatting her hand as she thrust it towards his face. 'Tully!' he yelled at the henchman bundling out from the tavern door. 'I don't pay you to stand by while I have to deal with crazed fans. Get this creature off me.'

Tully pushed the woman back towards the wall, and as Barbu marched away the strange woman melted back into the shadows from whence she had come.

CHAPTER 16

'**W**ilma Tenderfoot!' yelled Mrs Waldock, waddling into the doorway of her sitting room. 'I've been calling you for half an hour! Where have you been?'

Wilma, who had been awake all night making herself a Clue Board, scampered up to the hallway. She knew she was in trouble, and Pickle, who was far from stupid despite appearances to the contrary, knew it too, so as Wilma hurried towards the sitting room he trotted off to the kitchen. If he could stare nonchalantly in the direction of a pot of vegetable peelings and go unnoticed for long enough, then he might escape a roasting.

Wilma was panting from running up the cellar stairs. 'Never before!' wailed Mrs Waldock, spit cascading from her lips. 'Never before have I been sent a child so wilful! Why are you standing there with your cheeks puffed out? Stop pulling faces and deliver this letter. And when you've done that there's a sack of onions that needs peeling, and when you've done that you can file my toenails. And look sharp, Wilma Tenderfoot! Or I shall have you put in a box and sent back to that Institute quicker than you can count to ten!'

Wilma was skating on thin ice. If she was sent away now, her detective dreams would never come true. And as a general rule, small, fidgety but determined girls in the employ of large, irascible women should do as they are told, but Wilma, who was so bubbling over with clues and half-baked deductions, could only think of one thing: how to follow the world's greatest detective to Visser Haanstra's workshop. It would be the perfect opportunity to practise her eavesdropping – top tip number four. This time she'd get it right and Mr Goodman would just have to take her on.

Wilma's home-made Clue Board was as near to being like Detective Goodman's as she could manage, but without photos or blueprints or string it was a patchwork of torn-out pieces from the *Early Worm* newspaper around a navy-blue sock with the word VAULT written on it in chalk. Wilma looked up at it as she pulled on her hat to go to the post office. 'We must remember to write everything down so we don't forget it, Pickle,' she said to the beagle, who had followed her back down into their cellar. 'There was the thing about the lavender. Which almost certainly

means something. And the fish scale. Which might. And Visser
and his sugar – and some poison. Then there was the thing about
the frozen hearts. Which I can't work out. Maybe it's something
to do with bees, who like lavender and can sting? And what if
there's a special breed of bee that can sting ice? And might look
like this?' While Wilma was thinking aloud she was drawing a picture of a giant ice-stinging bee on the back of the envelope Mrs
Waldock had given her to post. Pickle, who had no idea what his
companion was rattling on about, stood very still. As a general
rule, if a dog is in doubt, that's what they do. Nothing at all.

'It's like that case when Mr Goodman caught the scientist who was breeding poisonous worms. Look here,' went on Wilma, flapping the relevant newspaper article on her Clue Ring. 'It's like that. But with bees. And ice stings. What do you think?'

She looked down at her faithful hound who quickly decided that standing stiller than he'd ever stood before was the only way out of this one.

Theodore P. Goodman, the world's greatest detective, was taking care not to touch anything. Crime scenes, whether they involved the theft of something small, like a paper clip, or the murder of something enormous, like a hippopotamus, deserved to be treated with solemnity. Having found Visser dead on the workshop floor, Theodore was keen to simply stand and look about him. The great detective liked to do this in an atmosphere of quiet contemplation but, with Inspector Lemone standing behind him, that was verging on the impossible.

'Slug stew, Goodman,' the Inspector was saying, pointing towards the pot on the floor. 'Never cared for it. Too chewy. Mind you, haven't had any lunch yet. Only had kippers and bacon for breakfast. And that cupcake. And those biscuits. And that sandwich. Bit peckish. Oh, and I had that pie. But all the same . . . Wonder if the slug stew's still warm . . .'

'Don't touch anything, please, Inspector,' murmured the

detective, stopping the Inspector by the arm as he bent down to stick his finger into the pot. 'Plenty of time for snacks. Someone, it would seem, is trying to cover their tracks. Witnesses are being eliminated.'

'Standard evil procedure.' The Inspector nodded, still staring at the stew. Then he got out his notebook to make it look as if he was actually doing something and secretly drew a small picture of someone who looked suspiciously like Mrs Speckle.

Theodore had moved over to the body and, having established that there were signs of a violent struggle, bent down to take a closer look. 'Interesting,' he said, peering at Visser through his magnifying glass. 'This man was beaten, but that was not how he died. Blood vessels about the mouth are broken. Some sort of poison . . .'

'Get away from him,' shouted a voice, suddenly, from behind them. Theodore stood and turned around. There in front of them was a small boy with a mop of curly brown hair and eyes that were bloodshot and teary. 'Don't touch him! Leave us alone!'

The great detective, quickly reading the situation for what it was, took a small step forward. 'Was this your father?' he asked, gently reaching out to put a hand on the boy's shoulder. Janty nodded and stared down at his tatty shoes. 'Did you see who did this?' Theodore asked carefully.

'No.' Janty sniffled, wiping a hand across his eyes. 'He always told me to hide when we had trouble. I was outside.'

'Is your mother here?' enquired Theodore, shooting a quick glance around him.

'Haven't got a mother,' mumbled Janty. 'I haven't got anyone now.'

'What's your name, young man?' asked the detective softly.

'Janty,' replied the boy, responding to Theodore's kindness. 'Janty Haanstra.'

'Janty,' began the detective, hand still on the boy's shoulder, 'I am very sorry for your loss. I will do my utmost to bring whoever did this to justice. But for now we need to get you away from here. Inspector,' he added, turning to his colleague, 'see to it that this boy is looked after. And take my handkerchief, Lemone. Dry your eyes, for goodness sake.'

'Much obliged,' sobbed the Inspector, who had a terrible weakness for bursting into tears wherever small children and bad news were concerned.

'Oh!' said a voice from the doorway. 'It's appalling. I couldn't believe the news. My old friend . . . dead?'

Theodore turned, his jaw setting to granite as he heard a voice he knew all too well. 'Barbu D'Anvers,' he whispered.

'Hello, Theodore,' said the tiny villain with a sneer. 'How perfectly ghastly to see you.'

Inspector Lemone thrust his notebook away and stuck his chest out. 'Now steady on, D'Anvers,' he blustered, wagging a finger in the criminal's direction. 'We'll have no unpleasantness here.'

'It's all right, Inspector,' said Theodore, raising a hand to stop his friend. 'But I am surprised to see you, Barbu. Don't tell me this grubby mess is your doing?'

Barbu frowned. 'Me? How could I? Visser was my very dearest friend. I have merely come to extend my commiserations and to take Janty home. Come, boy. Get your things. It's what your father wanted.'

'But I never met you,' complained Janty, staring at the black-clad figure before him. 'I never even heard of you.'

Barbu blinked. 'Never heard of me?' He asked, bending forward a little. 'But I am Barbu D'Anvers, the greatest criminal mind that ever lived. Tully! Give him a poster. Never heard of me indeed.'

Tully reached into his coat and unravelled a large poster of Barbu standing looking evil in front of a menacing skyline with the words 'Be Bad! Stay Bad!' emblazoned across the bottom.

'I can sign that for you if you like,' added Barbu, raising an eyebrow. Janty shook his head.

'What are you up to, Barbu?' asked Theodore, eyes narrowing. 'You've never shown a scrap of kindness in your life. What

do you want with this boy? He's going nowhere until I've got to the bottom of this.'

'Sorry!' said Barbu, grabbing Janty by the forearm. 'No time for that! We've got to get back. And seeing as how I am now the legal guardian of the boy, I can't possibly leave him with strangers.'

'What do you mean legal guardian?' spluttered the Inspector.

'Paperwork, Tully!' demanded the villain, clicking his fingers.

The henchman passed his master a folded piece of paper, which Barbu flicked open with a flourish. 'I hereby declare,' began the villain, reading out loud, 'that Barbu D'Anvers (that's me) has been declared the sole protector of Janty Haanstra, an orphan (that's you), until such time as . . . blah blah . . . and so it goes on. All above board.'

'Give that to me!' puffed the Inspector, grabbing the paper out of Barbu's hands. 'Well I never, Goodman, it's true. It's got the official stamp of the Lowside Institute for Woeful Children. They deal with all the island's orphans.'

'Wait a minute,' said Theodore, sensing foul play. 'How did you know Janty was an orphan, Barbu?'

A slow, evil smirk slithered across Barbu's lips. 'Well,' he said, with an arrogant twirl of his cane, 'nothing travels faster than bad news.'

'But I don't know you!' complained Janty again, pulling his

arm away from Barbu's grip. 'And besides, this man said he'd have me looked after. And he's going to find who killed my father!'

For a moment Barbu's eyes hardened. Then he lowered his head theatrically. 'Oh dear!' He grasped at his chest. 'You want to go with this man? This man who is responsible for all our miseries and disappointments? You do know who he is? You must do. Every Criminal Element on Cooper hates him. This, dearest boy, is Theodore P. Goodman. He was your father's mortal enemy!'

Janty twisted round to look up at the detective. 'You're Theodore P. Goodman?' he whispered, face contorting with confusion.

'Yes, he is!' shouted Wilma, leaping in from the corridor. 'And he's the greatest detective in the world!'

'Oh no, not again!' Theodore groaned. 'How did you get here?'

'The address of the workshop is mentioned in that report on the Case of the Silver Mask,' babbled Wilma quickly, 'and then I snuck across the border by hiding in the back of a cabbage cart. We smell a bit. Sorry.' Pickle looked delighted.

'How long have you been here?' demanded Theodore, being as serious as he could without losing his temper.

'I heard everything. I was practising eavesdropping – though I know that means I probably shouldn't have jumped out and

revealed myself . . .' Wilma acknowledged as the detective raised his eyebrows. 'But never mind that! We've got to stop the boy! You mustn't go with Barbu D'Anvers!' Wilma implored Janty. 'He's a very bad man. I've got loads of proof on my Clue Ring!'

'Who is this?' asked Barbu, stepping forward to glower at the determined ten-year-old. 'Is this girl a friend of yours, Janty?'

'Never seen her in my life,' the boy shrugged, still glaring at Theodore.

'Then this is clearly none of your business,' snapped the tiny villain to Wilma. 'Go away.'

Wilma gulped and said the first thing that came into her head which, for future reference, probably wasn't the best idea. 'I'm Wilma Tenderfoot. You're a lot shorter in real life,' she said. 'I mean, shorter than the pictures of you on my Clue Ring. I mean, in this one,' she rambled on, fumbling to find one of her newspaper scraps, 'you must be standing on a box or something.'

'Tully!' yelled the villain, eyes widening. 'Get her! Get her now, please!'

'Wilma!' shouted Theodore, striding out to stop Tully as he lumbered towards the ten-year-old girl. 'Get behind the Inspector. I shall talk to you in a moment. Janty, I know that right now you're having trouble trusting me, but here, take my card. You may need it.'

Theodore reached into his pocket and handed the small boy a card with his address on it. Janty stared at it, his grubby fingers smudging its edges. He had two choices: he could leave with Barbu and pursue the life he was born to or he could turn his back on everything his father stood for and believed in. Anger burned deep in Janty's heart. More than anything he wanted revenge, and as he stood, gazing at the card Theodore had given him, he realized that with it every ambition he had ever had would be thwarted. Janty had made his choice. Eyes flashing, he very slowly tore the card in two. Wilma gasped. 'I shan't be needing this now,' said Janty, in a low defiant mumble. 'I was born bad. And I'll stay bad.'

'But he's evil!' yelled Wilma, pointing towards Barbu. 'You can't want to be like him.'

'On the contrary,' sneered Barbu, placing a hand on Janty's shoulder. 'Everyone loves a bad boy. You'll understand when you're older. Tully, Janty, we're leaving.'

As they swept out Wilma bent down to pick up the torn pieces of card. 'I can't believe he did that, Mr Goodman,' she said with a shake of her head.

'This is a worrying development,' said Theodore, thinking out loud. 'But, Wilma, you shouldn't have come here. Being a detective isn't a game.'

'I know that, Mr Goodman,' said Wilma, twisting the end of

her pinafore. 'Oh my!' she added, glancing into the workshop. 'Is that a dead body?'

'Oooh,' murmured the Inspector. 'Probably shouldn't look at that. Being so young and all.'

'I don't mind, Inspector,' said Wilma. 'I saw a dead cat once. I'm not frightened. And besides, I have to get used to death, what with my going to be a detective and everything.'

'All the same,' said Theodore, 'there are some things you should be spared. Now then, Inspector, a word if I may.'

Wilma stood staring at the lifeless shape on the floor. She told herself she didn't have time to feel afraid; there was work to be done. As Theodore and the Inspector chatted in the corridor, Wilma wandered in to the workshop to take a closer look. Pickle, who had scampered ahead of her to explore that intriguing smell of stew, was pawing at something under the cooker, his nose glued to the floor. Wilma bent down to see what it was. It looked like the broken end of what seemed to be a dart. 'Well done, Pickle!' she whispered to the beagle. 'This looks like it could be important. We should show this to Mr Goodman! On the other hand . . .' added Wilma, thinking, 'perhaps I should try to find out what it is on my own. And prove myself to Mr Goodman that way – since the eavesdropping didn't quite work! I'll

just pop it in my pocket and have a closer look when we get back to Mrs Waldock's. Oh! Mrs Waldock's letter!' Wilma gasped. 'I totally forgot!' But just as she was about to dash off to deliver it, the detective approached, looking stern. 'The Inspector and I are heading back to Clarissa Cottage. We need to update the Clue Board, see where we're at. And you are going to come with us.'

'Oooh!' Wilma replied, eyes widening. 'Am I going to help you with some deductions and contemplating?'

'No, young lady,' answered Theodore, frowning. 'I am going to have a serious chat with you. A very serious chat indeed.'

Oh dear. That doesn't sound good, does it?

CHAPTER 17

Wilma's mind was whirring with thoughts and theorems: the small, feathery dart shaft in her pocket was clearly important, but without any time to sit down, contemplate it, make deductions and write things up on her Clue Board she was at sixes and sevens. Not only that, but as she followed Detective Goodman and the Inspector she was more than aware that she had a chore to do. A chore that wasn't getting done.

Wilma's eyes sparkled suddenly. 'Hang on,' she said, whispering down to Pickle. 'I should be concentrating on detective matters and darts, not having to post silly letters! And what Mrs Waldock doesn't know, Mrs Waldock can't get angry about. Letters get lost all the time don't they, Pickle?'

Pickle who, at that precise moment, had a small but nevertheless persistent itch in his left ear, shook his head and gave a little snort. 'That's what I think too,' said Wilma, with a nod. 'So

if I happened to lose this letter between here and Mrs Waldock's house, then that wouldn't necessarily be a bad thing, would it?'

And so the pair of them trotted after Cooper's greatest and most serious detective. And somewhere, between Visser Haanstra's workshop and the border with the Farside, Mrs Waldock's letter was inadvertently dropped under a gooseberry bush where no one was able to give it a second thought. How very convenient.

'I can't work it out, Goodman,' said Inspector Lemone as they approached the Border Control booth. 'Barbu D'Anvers is rotten to the core. What does he want – taking that young boy in? I don't like the smell of it. Something's not right.'

Theodore reached into his pocket for his Border Pass. 'That boy must know something useful,' he explained. 'Barbu obviously thinks so, anyway. And he wants the boy close, where we can't get to him. Ahh! Trevor! Good day to you.'

'Inspector,' replied Trevor, giving his cap a small tug. 'Mr Goodman. Just give your passes a stamp. Oh! That's your tenth one this week. That means you can have a . . . hang on, just check with the peepers . . .' A small note was handed up. 'Oooh!' exclaimed Trevor happily. 'A set of steak knives!'

'Hello, Trevor,' said Wilma, stepping up to the booth and trying to look official. 'I don't have a pass, but I'm with them.

Good day to you. Thank you. Come on, Pickle.'

Trevor stared down and spluttered. 'No pass? Hold on! Aren't you that girl who waved and questioned? Oh dear me no. No, no, no. No pass? Well! I thought I'd seen everything!' Another piece of paper appeared from the hole in the wall and was waved with some urgency. Trevor took it. 'As I suspected,' he said, glancing down. 'You've been given a Cheek-of-It Order. Only the very brazen get one of those. You're going nowhere.'

Theodore quickly approached the booth. 'Trevor,' he began, in as reasonable a manner as he could muster, 'am I right in thinking that ten stamps on my pass also entitle me to take a guest into the Farside?'

Another piece of paper was handed up.

Oh no, he's right.
Signed Kevin and Malcolm and Susan and IAN.
(Official Border-Control Peepers)

Trevor blinked. 'Hmmm. Annoying. But yes, Mr Goodman, it seems it does.'

'Good,' answered Theodore with a firm nod. 'Then come along, Wilma. Into the Farside we go.'

And as Wilma passed through, she couldn't help but shoot Trevor a smile that some would call smug. And Trevor, on seeing it, made a mental note that the next time he saw her he would make her wait for longer than anyone had ever had to wait before. Just see if he didn't.

Once back at Clarissa Cottage Theodore was ready to get straight down to business. 'Aah!' he declared as they all marched into his study. 'Mrs Speckle. Tea! And biscuits! Thank you!'

Wilma, finding herself back in her hero's study, was quietly bubbling with excitement. Maybe the serious chat he wanted to have with her was about making her his apprentice? What else could it be? She wandered over to the Clue Board and tried to appear serious. This was a momentous moment and she wanted to look prepared. Pickle, picking up on Wilma's portentous mood, licked his nose and sat up straight at her feet.

As Mrs Speckle padded into the study Inspector Lemone flushed a little and made his way over to the fireplace, where he stood with one hand on the mantelpiece. It might seem odd that he did this, but the fact was, he had read in a magazine that gentlemen can often look at their best when they assume manly poses and stare off into the middle distance. Theodore glanced over at his portly friend and gave a curious smile but said nothing. Sometimes friends just have to be left to pickle their own eggs.

'Note's been sent over from the Museum, Mr Goodman,' said Mrs Speckle, paying no attention to the Inspector. 'I've left it on the tray.'

'Thank you, Mrs Speckle,' said the detective, reaching for the handwritten letter and opening it.

'Are those new wellington boots you're wearing, Mrs Speckle?'

Mrs Speckle looked up from under her double bobble hats, glanced at the Inspector, who was standing very strangely, looked down at her boots and said, 'No.' Then, catching sight of Wilma, with Pickle at her heels, Mrs Speckle, who was deeply suspicious of small, determined girls, gave a tut of disapproval and muttered something under her breath that certainly doesn't need to be repeated here. As soon as she was gone, the Inspector stopped trying to hold his stomach in and wandered over to Theodore's desk.

'The Curator wants to see us later this afternoon,' said Theodore, reading from the letter. 'He wants an update on our progress with the case. We'll need to prepare a report. Oh . . . you've . . . eaten both the corn crumbles, Lemone. Again.'

'Could have sworn they were new wellingtons,' mumbled the Inspector, staring off in the direction of the doorway.

'Mr Goodman!' Wilma burst out suddenly, unable to keep quiet any longer. 'The thing is, it's like when Mr Hankley, the

baker, makes cakes for Mrs Waldock. He wouldn't make the cake unless Mrs Waldock had ordered it, which she did, and so the thing is, someone must have ordered the forger to make the fake stone because no one bakes a cake unless someone wants it . . .'

Theodore held out his hand. 'Slow down, Wilma,' he said, gesturing to a stool. 'I have something very serious to say to you. Try as I might, I clearly haven't managed to shake you off.'

Wilma nodded. 'Well, I can be quite sticky,' she said, ignoring the stool and bouncing around in front of Theodore's desk. 'Because once when you gave an interview you said great detectives should always be determined and perspirant.'

'Persistent,' corrected Theodore. 'Well, you're certainly that. But the thing is, Wilma, you are following the Inspector and me around when you shouldn't. You are Mrs Waldock's housegirl. You are not my apprentice.'

'Not yet I'm not, no,' said Wilma, with a shake of her head. 'But I've been doing the top tips and—'

'Wilma,' interrupted the great detective, 'this has to stop. The Inspector and I are trying to investigate a very serious case and we cannot be worrying about where and when you're going to pop up next.'

Wilma looked over at the Inspector for support, but his head was hanging down as if he didn't want to catch her eye.

'So that's that,' added Theodore, getting out his note-book. 'No more chasing us around, Wilma. Do you understand?'

It wasn't in Wilma's nature to be silent, but somehow, at that moment, no words would come. Her chest felt as if it had filled with lead and there was a large, uncomfortable lump in her throat.

'I'd offer you a corn crumble before you go, of course,' said Theodore, realizing that Wilma was upset. 'But sadly,' he added, throwing his friend a sideways glance, 'the Inspector has eaten them all.'

'Didn't mean to,' mumbled Inspector Lemone, still looking at his shoes. 'Just sort of happened.'

'Don't worry,' said Wilma quietly. 'I'm not hungry now anyway.'

'Hmmm, well then,' said Theodore, twiddling his moustache awkwardly. 'Off you go. I'd better be getting on with the assignment for the Curator.'

Wilma cocked her head to one side and scrunched up her nose. 'An a-sigh-what?'

'An assignment,' explained the great detective, hooking his thumbs into his waistcoat pockets. 'It's like a project. But more official. The Curator is due here in a few hours and he's sent me a note asking for a written report that details what we have

discovered so far: clues, information and suspects, that sort of thing. Anyway . . . I am very busy and—'

'Is it a bit like when it was laundry day at the Institute and I had to write down how many pants went missing?' said Wilma, not wanting to leave.

Theodore blinked. 'Not really,' he said, after a short pause. 'Although in terms of being a summary of what has happened then I suppose the two are vaguely similar.'

'Very vaguely,' added the Inspector, bending down to give Pickle a pat.

'Oh, wait. You wrote about an assignment when you solved the Case of the Missing Wig,' blurted Wilma, reaching for her Clue Ring. 'I think I've got it here . . .'

'Wilma,' said Theodore P. Goodman softly, getting out of his chair and walking towards the ten-year-old, 'you must go home now.' The world-famous and very serious detective stood and looked down at the small but determined girl in front of him. Her eyes were pricking with tears and she was knotting the bottom of her pinafore with her hands. 'You really do want to be a detective, don't you?' he asked, putting a hand on her shoulder.

'It's all I ever wanted, Mr Goodman,' she whispered, looking up at her hero. 'Not just to solve cases and everything. But also so I can work out where I've come from. And things . . .' Her voice trailed off.

'And your determination is to be admired, but this really is for the best,' Theodore said gruffly.

'Come, come,' said Inspector Lemone sadly, seeing Wilma's face. 'Whenever I feel a few tears coming on I try gulping three times. Always seems to do the trick.'

'Well then, Wilma,' said Theodore, in an important voice, 'let's shake hands and say goodbye.'

'Goodbye?' asked Wilma, but before she could quite take it all in she felt Theodore's hand in hers and somehow she was leaving his study, possibly forever. Wilma couldn't believe what was happening and, because it really was all a bit too much, she gulped six times. (Just to make sure.)

CHAPTER 18

Dark corners should always be avoided, everyone knows that, and as Wilma and Pickle, miserable and crestfallen, trudged back up the steps of Howling Hall, there was one dark corner they would have done well to steer clear of. Mrs Waldock, like a malevolent predator, was lying in wait.

With a heavy heart Wilma closed the front door behind her. Detective Goodman had been quite clear: she wasn't allowed to help with the case. At every turn she had failed to prove herself as a detective's apprentice. Taking off her raggedy cloth cap and pushing the hair from her eyes, she looked down at the luggage tag in her hand, the only clue to her past and one she was desperate to solve. 'I *will* be a detective one day, Pickle,' she murmured. 'I have to be. Mr Goodman was right. I am very determined and maybe, if I . . .' But Wilma didn't have a chance to finish her thoughts. Suddenly, out from the shadow of the

broken grandfather clock in the hallway, came a pair of fleshy, grasping hands. As her mistress grabbed her by the throat, Wilma let out a scream. 'Wilma Tenderfoot,' hissed Mrs Waldock, tightening her grip, 'you have scampered at will once too often. The time has come for you to be punished with the worst chore imaginable.'

'But, Mrs Waldock . . .' gasped Wilma, clutching at her mistress's hand. 'I was just delivering your letter!'

'Too late for that!' shouted Mrs Waldock, her cheeks wobbling with rage. 'You will go into the sitting room and collect every single spider until you have enough to make me some spider-leg soup!' Wilma, tossed in the direction of the sitting room, stumbled to the floor, and as she scrabbled to her feet her precious luggage tag fell from her grasp.

'What's this?' barked Mrs Waldock, picking it up.

'It's mine!' yelled Wilma. 'Give it back!'

'Give it back?' shouted Mrs Waldock, thumping Wilma on the back of the head. 'No housegirl tells me what to do! I'm keeping it! Now get collecting! This is your last chance! And not one sound . . . or I shall give you the thrashing you deserve!'

Pickle, his tail firmly between his legs, crawled into the sitting room behind Wilma. 'Well, this is a mess,' whispered Wilma, pinching her lips together bravely. 'I'll have to get my luggage

tag back. Maybe we can wait till she's asleep. Ugh!' she added, scrunching her face into a picture of disgust. 'There are cobwebs everywhere. And I HATE spiders!'

Those of you who have tried to catch a spider will know that they are fiendishly quick, and as Wilma peered into revolting nooks and mildewed crannies, she had to conclude that having eight legs rather than two seemed to be giving the spiders the advantage. After an hour of trying to grab even one Wilma was sweating and exhausted. But at least it was keeping her mind off her horrible disappointments. As Wilma took a breather, Pickle, who had thrown in the occasional threatening bark (a contribution rendered useless by the fact that spiders are totally deaf) was bouncing round the room and sniffing, nose glued to the ground in the hope of rooting out more quarry. He had almost given up when suddenly a particularly fat and hairy spider came into his line of vision. His tail went up, his back became rigid and with one, overenthusiastic pounce, he bounded into a pot stand, sending the plant and a framed photograph smashing to the floor. 'Oh, Pickle, no!' Wilma cried out, clamping a hand to her mouth.

'What was that noise?' bellowed Mrs Waldock, silhouetted in the doorway.

Wilma was already picking up the pieces of glass from the photo frame. She glanced at the picture in her trembling hands.

It was of a man and glitzily dressed woman, cheek-to-cheek and laughing. Wilma squinted and held the photo up to look at it better. Could the woman be a slimmer, younger Mrs Waldock? And who was the grinning fellow beside her? 'I'm sorry, Mrs Waldock,' she stuttered as her mistress loomed over her.

Wilma braced herself, expecting a beating, but Mrs Waldock, seeing the picture in Wilma's hands, seemed, for a moment, to crumple. Some people spend their whole lives trying to forget, so when they are presented with the very thing they have been avoiding, the shock can be overwhelming. Wilma looked up. If the room hadn't been so dark she might have concluded that there were tears in her mistress's eyes, but surely that wasn't possible? 'You will take this,' mumbled Mrs Waldock, 'and have it reframed immediately. Have you caught any spiders?'

'No, I . . .' began Wilma, but Pickle gave her a nudge with his cold nose. Under his paw there was one squashed spider. 'What I mean to say is, I haven't caught one, but Pickle has.'

'Then you can make my soup on your return. Skip to it. We haven't got all day.' Mrs Waldock handed Wilma back the broken frame and wandered away, muttering as she went. 'Abandoned . . . all the money gone . . . said he'd come back . . .'

'What,' said Wilma, 'was that about? If I was still being a detective then I'd probably deduct that this man here,' she added, tapping the photo with a finger, 'was a wrong'un of the

155

highest order. Still. I'm not a detective now. I'm Mrs Waldock's housegirl. For the time being anyway. Well done for catching the spider, Pickle. I'll put it in my pocket.' Wilma reached down and peeled the flattened spider from the bottom of Pickle's paw. Pinching it between her forefinger and thumb, and with something of a grimace, she held open her pinafore pocket to drop it in. 'Pickle!' she yelled, looking into her pocket. 'The dart thing! I've still got it! I know Mr Goodman told me I wasn't to help him any more, but I have to give him this! It could be a vital clue.'

'To date,' Theodore began, 'we have no confirmed suspects. I'm awaiting test results from Dr Kooks. I'm hoping the poison that killed Visser will lead us somewhere. In fact, I'm heading to the lab now. Perhaps you'd like to come with me?'

Theodore was standing at the gate of Clarissa Cottage. The Curator and his assistant, Miss Pagne, were sitting in a smart brown buggy outside.

'Not possible,' huffed the Curator, holding on to his cane with both hands. 'Up to my eyes with whatnots and wherewithalls. That's why we can't stop. But what you're saying, Goodman, is that you know very little. This is not what I expect from a detective of your calibre. The Museum's reputation is at stake.'

'If anyone can solve this case, it's Theodore P. Goodman!' the

Inspector blustered, coming down the path behind the world-famous detective.

'Now now, Inspector,' Theodore said, packing his pipe with some rosemary tobacco. 'The Curator is within his rights to be anxious. But if we discover who killed Visser, I think we'll have our man.'

'Or woman,' said Miss Pagne, from behind the Curator's shoulder. She was wearing a tight, fitted purple dress with long white starched cuffs and a plunging neckline that gathered itself into an ostentatious bow at the centre of which was a ruby brooch that matched her painted fingernails.

'Indeed,' said Theodore, momentarily forgetting about the packing of his pipe. 'Although I would say it's unlikely.'

'Are you suggesting that women are incapable of great evil, Mr Goodman?' oozed the assistant, slowly crossing her legs.

'Suddenly feeling a bit warm,' said the Inspector, fiddling with his collar. 'I'll loosen my tie a bit.'

'On the contrary, Miss Pagne,' replied Theodore, paying no attention to his friend. 'To underestimate any woman is to tread a path of peril.'

Miss Pagne stared at the detective and let a small, wry smile dance across her lips. 'You're as perceptive as you are handsome, Mr Goodman,' she purred.

'Jolly hot today,' coughed the Inspector. 'Isn't it?'

'That'll do, Miss Pagne!' barked the Curator, giving the floor of the buggy a double thump with his cane. 'This is all very disappointing. Still. Nothing to be done until you've made some progress. Double your efforts, Goodman! I expect nothing less! But I must warn you, if I don't see results soon I shall pass this matter to Captain Brock and the army.'

'Captain Brock isn't a detective!' spluttered Inspector Lemone.

'But he produces results, Inspector!' shouted the Curator. 'Results which I'm not seeing from you!'

'I've got some results!' shouted a small, panting voice from the road behind them. 'And before you tell me off, Mr Goodman, I'm not chasing after you or anything. But I have got something I should have given you before. Pickle found it at the workshop. I wanted to make some deductions of my own before I gave it to you. But I guess I'm not allowed to do that now. And what with it being a vital clue and everything, it's only right that you should have it. Anyway, here it is.' She held out her hand and opened it. As she did so, Miss Pagne screamed.

'A spider?' asked the Curator, staring at the insect in Wilma's hand.

'Argh!' yelled Wilma, flicking the squashed thing back into her pocket. 'No. Not that. This. It's a piece of broken dart.'

'Let me see,' said Theodore, striding forward to take a look, his magnifying glass in hand. 'Look at that, Mr Curator. Light-

158

ly feathered with a pointed wooden shaft. A blow dart. Quite crudely made.'

'But effective,' said the Curator, taking the dart shaft and peering at it.

'So someone,' said the Inspector, rubbing his chin, 'blew a poisoned dart at Visser? Presumably to avoid being seen. But from where?'

'There was an air vent,' pondered Theodore. 'Up on the right-hand wall. The angle from there would have been perfect to dispatch the dart. But that's not all this means. It now seems likely that whoever beat Visser up – and I'm beginning to recognize the handiwork of Barbu D'Anvers here –WASN'T the one to poison him . . .'

'So someone came in the door and someone else must have crawled down the vent!' urged Wilma. 'Not that I'm deducting or anything. I'm too busy getting this picture reframed. Pickle broke it. Mrs Waldock's sent me out.'

'Mrs Waldock?' asked the Curator, with a squint.

'She's my mistress,' explained Wilma, pointing at her in the broken picture. 'Although, to be honest, she looks a lot different from that these days. Still, I'm definitely doing my chores now, Mr Goodman! All the same, I bet if you followed that air vent to where it started there might be a whole bag of clues!'

'It's a basic deduction, Wilma,' said Theodore. 'Vents can start

in many places. But have you seen that feather, Mr Curator? Pale blue with golden flecks. Very unusual. This is an excellent clue.' He paused and cleared his throat. 'Well done, Wilma.'

Wilma flushed with delight. At last she had managed to find a proper clue. Even if it was more Pickle's doing. She gave the beagle a grateful wink. And more importantly, Detective Goodman was pleased with her! She'd show him she could be his apprentice yet!

The Curator looked distastefully down his stubby nose at Wilma, who gave him one of her stares. 'Yes, well,' he said, putting the dart down on a plate of corn crumbles that Inspector Lemone had left resting on the side arm of the buggy. 'I suppose this is something approaching a development. But we still don't have our man, Goodman!'

'Despite this young girl's efforts,' whispered Miss Pagne, shooting Wilma a sideways glance.

Wilma looked up at the glamorous assistant and felt a little uncomfortable. She wasn't used to the company of attractive ladies. She was more accustomed to battleaxes and heffalumps. Wilma glanced down at herself. Her pinafore was creased and grubby and she had some tufts of grass sticking out of one sock. 'I've been catching spiders,' she explained with another defiant stare, catching Miss Pagne's unimpressed eye.

'Never fear, Mr Curator!' enthused the Inspector. 'Now

we've got that dart, Goodman will have this wrapped up quicker than a Christmas present! He'll work out how it was made and where it came from and so forth. That dart will give us some answers! Just see if it doesn't!'

'No, Pickle, no!' yelled Wilma suddenly. As they had all stood about, the resourceful hound, sniffing a half-eaten corn crumble, had crept up to the edge of the buggy, jumped on to the footplate and snaffled the abandoned biscuit, and with it the shattered dart shaft, lying on the plate next to the biscuit, had vanished. Pickle had eaten the evidence.

'Why is it,' wailed Wilma, 'that every time I try to do something right, it always ends up going wrong?'

But no one had an answer to that.

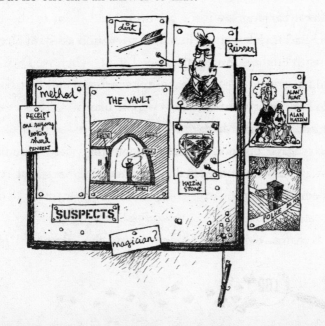

CHAPTER 19

'Yes!' declared Barbu, throwing a hand into the air. 'I think those colours suit you perfectly!'

Janty, in a pair of bottle-green shorts and a custard-yellow jumper, was standing on a box looking miserable, his mass of dark curls hanging low over his eyes. 'Add them to the pile, please,' Barbu yelled at the hunched-over shop assistant already laden with clothes. 'And get changed, Janty. Then we shall buy you an ice cream. Or milkshake. Or whatever it is that young people like. Tully, what do young people like?'

'Smoking cigars, Mr Barbu?'

Barbu gave his henchman a penetrating stare. 'Smoking cigars . . .' he mumbled, shaking his head. 'Honestly, I don't know why I bother.'

The Bravura department store was the Farside's most

magnificent shop. Shaped like a giant aniseed twist, from the floors and the pillars to the counters and the tills everything was made of glass so that you could stand on the second floor and see all the way up to the fifth and back down to the basement. Barbu had brought Janty to children's clothing on the third floor, past the glass Fountain of Fizz, where bubbly drinks shot out at passers-by at random intervals. Tully had just been sprayed with a particularly sticky splodge of raspberry and treacle cola and was still trying to scrape the gloopy mess from the inside of his nose. It was exactly the kind of chirpy place that Barbu hated, but he had a plan and knew what he was doing. Charm the boy and he would get what he wanted: the secret of who had ordered the fake Katzin stone.

As a general rule, children should never trust grown-ups who want to buy them lots of gifts. Adults are selfish creatures and despite their having access to things children don't, like bank overdrafts, sudden displays of generosity should be treated with nothing but suspicion. In most cases they just want you to shut up, but sometimes, as here, they're after something more sinister.

'I know these trinkets are an inadequate recompense for your loss,' trilled Barbu softly, putting a black-clad arm about Janty's shoulder, 'but if there is anything I can do for you . . . anything at all . . .' He trailed off and, turning his head away, sniffed a little.

'Your father was a good man and a great forger. The best. If only there was some way of continuing his work . . . of honouring him . . . to maybe have some sort of memorial . . . for all those he knew. But it's no good. He was so secretive. Nature of the business, I suppose . . . but if I could just find out who his clients were . . . if there was, oh I don't know . . . an order book . . .'

Barbu snapped his head back round to stare at Janty. The boy looked up. It was the first time he had ever heard anyone talk fondly of his father and his watery grey eyes flickered with gratitude. 'Did you really like my dad?' he asked.

'Oh!' exclaimed Barbu, throwing back his head. 'Like him? I ADORED him! And so brilliantly talented! He could make anything from . . . well, anything!'

'What did he make for you?' continued Janty.

'What did he make for me?' whispered Barbu, with a blink. 'What DID he make for me? Well. He made . . . umm . . . he made . . . no! I can't speak of it! It's too painful! Let me just remember it in my own mind. Yes. There. I've remembered it. Sort of funny-shaped. With a thing. Good.'

'My father wanted me to be a forger too,' said Janty. 'He was teaching me everything he knew before he . . .' But the words caught in his throat and his chin fell back down on to his chest. 'I can't believe someone killed him! Who would do such a thing? And why?'

'There, there,' said Barbu, pushing his bottom lip out. 'We must be strong. We both miss him. TERRIBLY. Of course your father would be delighted that I am now your guardian. Thank goodness we arrived in time to save you from the dreadful do-gooder Theodore P. Goodman. Awful man, isn't he, Tully?'

'Well, I've only met him a few times,' answered the big idiot, putting a finger to his lips to help him think. 'And to be honest . . . oww!' The silver fist of Barbu's cane thwacked off Tully's forehead.

'Never mind,' snapped Barbu. 'All Janty needs to know is that we are his new family now. And family share things. What is mine is yours. Except the things in the blue cupboard in my study. They're not yours. But everything else — fine. And what is yours . . . is mine. So you said your father had an order book . . . ?'

'Did I?' sniffled Janty, rubbing his eyes dry. 'I don't remember.'

'Well, think again,' replied Barbu, his tone hardening. 'It's very important. Your father would have wanted me to keep his secrets safe. Just as he trusted me to look after you. And I suspect,' added Barbu, with a cunning snarl, 'that whoever killed your father is probably in it.'

'My father did have an order book, yes,' answered the boy eventually, a little stunned by the sudden revelation. 'But he told me to hide it and never let anyone see it.'

'OBVIOUSLY that doesn't apply to me!' guffawed Barbu,

thumping Tully in the chest. 'As if! Ha ha ha! No. What he meant was, only show it to people you trust. And you trust me. Don't you, Janty?' The villain had crept in close, his words slithering like snakes. 'And you do want to find your father's killer . . .'

Janty looked down at the bags he was carrying. 'Well, you did buy me all these clothes . . . and I do want to find out who did it. More than anything.'

'Yes,' whispered the black-hearted villain. 'Yes, you do.'

'And you did save me from the police.'

'Yes,' whispered Barbu, closing his eyes and tilting his head. 'Yes, I did.'

'And if my father arranged for you to be my guardian then I suppose he trusted you.'

'Oh, he did, Janty. He trusted me very much.'

'Well, all right then,' said Janty, his head lifting. 'My father's order book is in a building on the edge of Under Welmed, on the Lowside. But I've hidden it. And only I know where it is.'

'Then we must find it before it falls into the wrong hands, my boy,' said Barbu, with a sense of triumphant urgency. 'Because THAT would never do!'

And off they swept, with Janty in the dark shadow of Barbu's cloak.

CHAPTER 20

Wilma was standing in the waiting area of Miss Dechrista's Framing Emporium with her arms folded. She had a ticket in one hand and was deep in thought. Pickle, head slumped, was sitting on the floor emitting occasional puffing noises. The pair of them were in trouble. And they knew it. 'Seeing as we've really mucked things up this time,' Wilma began, tapping the ticket against her top teeth, 'we ought to try to make things right.' Pickle hung his head to one side in an attempt to look penitent, but it was tricky – that biscuit had been extremely tasty.

'I mean, for a minute there, Mr Goodman was impressed, I know he was. But now he'll never have me as his apprentice if I don't fix things!' Wilma's eyes lit up. 'I really need to have another look at my Clue Board. Because we've got the dart stuff to add. Even if you did eat it.'

Wilma looked down at Pickle. He had tensed and had one paw in the air pointing towards the lane outside the shop. 'Pickle!' said Wilma, giving him a nudge. She followed his line of sight. There, striding towards them was Janty closely flanked by Barbu and Tully. Wilma gasped. 'Remember Mr Goodman's top tips? Number three: "Keep a sharp lookout for suspects and sometimes creep around after them!" This is our last chance to put things right! We have to follow them, Pickle, we can come back for the picture later.' The hound let out a small snort that sounded remarkably like 'Agreed'.

It was clear from the off that Janty was heading for the Lowside of the island. The cart depot was a short walk from the border village of Measly Down, and the shortcut the boy had taken from the Bravura department store had led the rotten troupe straight into Wilma's path. Luckily for Wilma and Pickle, the depot was always busy in the early evening, packed with people waiting for carts to take them back to the Lowside, and so the pair of them were able to blend into the crowd while still keeping an eye on their targets. Barbu, who wouldn't be seen dead in a public cart, booked his own private barouche to travel in. It was parked to the left of the depot, and seeing them climb in, Wilma realized she had to think fast.

'If I remember rightly,' whispered Wilma, bobbing behind a donkey, 'there's a lot of ducking and also diving involved in creeping around after suspects. It might help if we're slightly in disguise too. There's a couple of sacks of potatoes over there. If we put them on and things get precarious – that's a word that detectives use when situations take a turn for the worse, I found it in Mr Goodman's dictionary – we can just lie down and pretend to be bags of vegetables.'

Wilma snuck over to the potato bags and undid the tops. Tipping out the potatoes, she dragged the sacks to the nearest cart and, taking a small iron pick hanging on a hook at the back of the tailgate, poked out some eyeholes, slipped one sack over Pickle's head and lifted him into the back of the empty cart. 'Lie still,' she whispered, as she tugged the other sack over her own head and climbed in behind him. 'They're just ahead of us. When we get into the Lowside we can jump out and follow them again. But for now, pretend you're a potato.' Pickle gave a little huff. He'd never been a potato before and couldn't shake the feeling that imitating a small muddy tuber was a little bit undignified for a hound. Still, he had eaten that dart.

Twenty minutes later both cart and carriage had arrived on the Lowside at the village of Under Welmed. Wilma and Pickle slipped down, still wearing their sacks, and positioned themselves behind a water barrel. Dusk was drawing in, and with dark clouds gathering on the horizon Janty led Barbu and Tully through a graveyard on the edge of the village. The low evening sun was casting a bruised light and, as they picked their way through the tombstones, the three of them were at one with the shadows. They were heading for an abandoned windmill just north of the village, where no one but the crows gathered in the twilight. Wilma, poking her head over the top of a gravestone, peered through the holes in her sack. 'They're going into that crumbly building, Pickle,' she whispered. 'That's interesting. When Mr Goodman solved the Case of the Melted Motor, he said that, as a general rule, anyone heading into disused places was generally up to no good. We must creep very carefully. I think we might be on the verge of another clue.'

Pickle, who was struggling to track the villains from inside an oversized potato sack, tried to shake his head to show he'd understood, but all he succeeded in doing was getting one of his ears stuck in an eye hole. This was going to be a very long evening.

As Janty led Barbu and Tully in through the broken door of the windmill, he felt the sharp pang that goes hand in hand with being somewhere filled with memories. Everything around him seemed familiar yet distant, as if he was looking at his former life down the wrong end of a telescope. The milling room was a decrepit version of its former self: a large stone spur wheel was propped up against one wall, a broken grain hopper dangled from the bin floor above them and the ground was strewn with rusted tools. In a corner there was a heavy oak table, collapsed on one leg, and above it, on the wall, a few dusty pictures and ornaments. Barbu took in the room with a sneer and raised a hand to his nose. 'Ugh,' he sniffed. 'So dirty. And I can't be around wheat. Terribly bad for the complexion.'

'This was our hiding place, Mr D'Anvers,' said Janty, picking up a broom handle and tossing it across the room. 'No one comes here. Good meeting place too. For people who wanted to place orders in private.'

'Yes, well. Talking of that. Your father's book, Janty,' said Barbu, flicking his cloak behind him as he stood close to the boy's shoulder. 'Fetch it for me.'

'I hid my father's order book in our cleverest place. I designed it myself.' Janty walked towards the wall. On it hung a framed picture of a fish about to bite a worm on a hook. 'The fish thinks he's the hunter,' said Janty, looking back over his shoulder, 'but he's not. He's the hunted. It's a lesson my father taught me. When we think we are the hunters, sometimes we are the hunted. And because of that, everything must be protected.' Janty looked back at the painting and felt its surface with his fingertips. The hook that seemed so flat and lifeless rose up at Janty's touch and there was a popping noise as the fish slid out from the wall to

reveal a small rectangular tray. Janty put his hand into the drawer and pulled out a battered-looking book. He held it up. 'Here you are, Mr D'Anvers. My father's order book.'

Barbu strode forward and snatched it from the boy's hand. Triumphant, he waved it in the air. 'We have it, Tully!' he declared, eyes aflame. 'And with it we shall find out who ordered the fake Katzin Stone! And when we know that, the real one will be ours!'

'It'll never be yours!' yelled Wilma, leaping in through a tumble down window and pulling off her potato sack. 'That order book is official evidence and must be handed over in accordance with . . . hang on a minute,' she added, stopping to frantically thumb through her Clue Ring. 'The law! Yes! In accordance with the law! Pickle, get up! I know it's all gone precarious, but now isn't the time to lie down!'

Sometimes it might seem like a good idea to jump out on a known and wicked criminal but, for slightly untidy ten-year-old girls with no one except a small beagle struggling inside a sack to help them, leaping out on people completely lacking in morals is generally a bad idea. A very bad idea indeed.

Barbu fixed his eyes on the little girl in her pinafore standing in front of him and with an incredulous guffaw turned to Tully and said matter-of-factly, 'Well, if it isn't our little eavesdropper, Wilma Tenderfoot. Kill her, Tully. And her dog too.' Starting

for the door, he flung one corner of his cloak over his shoulder and said, 'Come along, Janty. No need for us to get our hands dirtier than they are already.'

'You mustn't give him the book, Janty!' Wilma cried out. 'He's a very bad man. Help me! Together we can get the book!'

'Why would I want to help you?' asked Janty, frowning. 'You're just a stupid goody-goody girl. I want to know who killed my father. And he's going to find out.'

'But—'

'Yes, I am,' Barbu smirked. 'Thus I win. Tully – get on with it.'

Tully lunged forward to grab at Wilma's dress, but as he did so Pickle, who had finally managed to wriggle his way out of the potato sack, leaped growling at the thug's hefty forearm and bit down hard. Letting out a yowl of pain, the henchman fell backwards into the stone spur wheel, sending it rocking towards Barbu and Janty. Wilma, sensing an opportunity, threw herself against the edge of the wheel too and heaved with all her might, sending the heavy stone structure crashing down on top of the villain and his young charge. As Barbu fell to the floor, the order book flew from his hand, rotated in the air and then fell downwards to land with a thud and skid across the windmill floor. Unable to move, Barbu shrieked at his sidekick 'There, Tully! Grab the book! Forget the dog! Grab the book!'

Wilma, diving after the sliding book, had just got a hand to

it when a thick fist came from nowhere and knocked her sideways. Dazed and thrown across the room, Wilma looked up once more to see Tully in possession of the order book. Pickle was still bravely attached to Tully's forearm, but the henchman was now spinning in a circle to rid himself of the determined hound, Pickle's legs and ears flapping as they went. Barbu was screaming orders and Janty was trying to wriggle free of the heavy milling wheel. He had almost got himself out. Wilma had to act quickly. She had landed at the base of a heap of old rusted tools and pans in a corner of the room and reaching up, she felt her hand hit a heavy iron pot. Pushing herself up from the floor she grabbed it and ran at Tully. As she ran she raised the pot above her head by its handle. Then with one almighty swing she thwacked him over the head. Tully stopped in mid-twirl, turned to see what had hit him and, with eyes rolling, slumped to the floor. Wilma, grabbing the order book from his hand, shouted at Pickle, 'Come on! I've got it! Not so stupid now, am I?' she added in Janty's direction as the boy stared after her with a curious look in his eye. She reached the door with the high-pitched screams of a livid Barbu D'Anvers ringing in her ears. 'If it's the last thing I do!' he wailed. 'I'll get you, Wilma Tenderfoot! I'LL GET YOU!'

And Wilma had no reason whatsoever not to believe him. Which was worrying.

CHAPTER 21

'Top tip number five!' yelled Wilma, as they ran at full speed. 'When escaping, be circuitous! I'm not quite sure what that means. Hang on. I'll look it up!' Pulling the dictionary out of her pinafore pocket as she ran, she quickly flipped the pages. 'It's an awfully big word!' she shouted back towards Pickle, who was hard on her heels. 'Circuitous! Taking the longer way round in order to avoid bumping into anyone that might want to kill you! That sounds like a good idea. Let's get on with it!'

The plucky pair scampered down side alleys, hopped over fences and zigzagged across fields. With Cooper's very worst villain on their tails, being circuitous seemed their best option. Having been circuitous for the best part of thirty minutes, Wilma and Pickle careered towards the brick wall that separated the two sides of the island. Wilma took a peek towards the Border Control station. Trevor's booth was empty. The coast was clear.

Somehow they had to get back to the Farside – and to Mr Goodman – but with the border now closed for the night they were in grave danger of being trapped. 'I need to think circuitously,' whispered Wilma, tapping her bottom lip with her index finger. 'We have to get across the border but not in a way that anyone would expect.'

Pickle pawed at Wilma's elbow and pointed his nose upwards. Wilma looked. There was a ladder hanging on a hook above them. 'Of course!' she said, giving the beagle a quick rub on the head. 'We can go over!' Wilma reached up and fetched the ladder. Leaning it in position, she took the ends of her pinafore and tied them round her neck so that the bottom of her dress formed a sort of sling. Then, lifting Pickle, she said, 'Don't wriggle,' and placed him inside the makeshift pouch. 'No licking either. It tickles.'

Steadily Wilma ascended the ladder, and Pickle, who was quietly enjoying the toasty confines of the makeshift sling, yawned a bit and allowed his thoughts to wander to bones and biscuits. Dogs, whenever they find themselves in a toasty environment, will immediately forget what it is they are supposed to be concentrating on. This is why they should never be left in warm rooms in charge of heavy machinery. And why Pickle didn't notice until too late that his cosy sling was gradually slipping lower and lower. For the knot at the back of Wilma's neck wasn't quite

done up tight enough and, at the top of the ladder, as Wilma put one hand on the tiled ledge of the wall, it finally came undone. The cradle, which had seemed so safe, gave way. 'Pickle!' yelled Wilma as the yelping hound fell downwards. She knew she had but a moment to save her faithful friend. Thinking quickly, she stuck her leg out, just catching his collar on the buckle of her sandal. She heaved a sigh of relief as Pickle, gently swaying on the end of her foot, tried not to look as startled as he felt. It was a lucky escape, but their troubles were far from over, for as Wilma lunged to catch Pickle she had lost her footing on the ladder, sending it clattering to the floor. The pair were dangling helplessly by her one hand from the top of the wall. 'Now what are we going to do? wailed Wilma. 'This is hopeless! Like when Mr Goodman solved the Case of the Shattered Spleen! He had to swing an anvil on to a rocky outcrop. If only I had an anvil! Or some sort of weight!' Pickle, still hanging by his collar, gave a short but significant snort. 'Hang on!' yelled Wilma, looking down, 'I've got you! If I use you as a weight, Pickle, I can swing you off the end of my shoe and on to the wall-ledge and then you can help pull me up! I can't think of anything else, can you?' And with that she swung her leg once, twice and then on the third swing up she flicked Pickle, who flew, ears akimbo, through the air and landed on the ledge above her. 'Now take hold of my sleeve and pull, Pickle, pull!' Wilma shouted, blinking upwards

at her dog. Pickle, still a little startled from his flight, gave his head a quick shake and then sunk his teeth into Wilma's shirt sleeve. As he pulled backwards, Wilma was able to get her other hand hooked over the ledge and between them, somehow, she scrabbled her way up on to the wall. 'Blimey,' she said, panting. 'Being circuitous isn't as easy as it sounds.'

'What about,' said Inspector Lemone, holding a finger in the air, 'if we had a snooze, you know, forty winks or so, because I read somewhere, can't think where, that sometimes people have their best ideas when they're asleep? I think they're called power naps or some such. Perhaps we could get Mrs Speckle to bake us a pie . . . you know . . . to help with the snoozing? And it is awfully late . . .'

Theodore P. Goodman, the world's greatest and most serious detective, was thumbing through a book, looking for the section on Blow Darts, and was paying little attention to the Inspector. 'Ahh,' he said, at last, tapping the relevant page. 'I thought as much! As I recall, the feather on that dart was a violet blue criss-crossed with gold. And the only bird with that colouration is . . .' The detective reached for another hefty book on his desk and opened it with a thump. 'Here! The Pippin Warbler! And where does it nest, Lemone?' he added triumphantly.

'Umm, in a tree?' answered the Inspector, who had already

started his snooze and was lying on the chaise longue with one eye open.

'Not just any tree, Inspector!' declared Theodore, standing up. 'The Cynta tree! The same tree whose poison was on that shard! And I'll bet, when we talk to forensics, the same tree whose poison killed Visser.' He began to scribble on his Clue Board.

'So it was a tree who stole the Katzin Stone?' mumbled the Inspector, who now had both eyes closed and was starting to dream of a land made of pies.

'No!' said Theodore, striding up and down. 'But it means that the person who made the dart also touched the fake Katzin Stone. As I suspected, they are one and the same, Lemone! Hmmm. There's only one Cynta tree on Cooper Island, and if I remember correctly,' he added, reaching for a large book of newspaper clippings, 'it's at the Hilbottom arboretum!'

'Arbor-what?' muttered the Inspector.

'Arboretum,' explained Theodore. 'Where trees are collected and nurtured. Aha!' He jabbed a finger at a newspaper photo of a special tree planting. 'And there it is! I think we've had our first breakthrough, Lemone! Hmmm,' he added, getting out his magnifying glass and looking a little closer at something. 'How interesting.'

'And I've got the second breakthrough!' panted Wilma,

pulling herself in through the window to the detective's study, Pickle fast behind her.

Theodore spun round. 'Wilma, why are you coming in through the window?'

'We've had to be circuitous,' Wilma explained, pausing to make sure he had registered that she'd accomplished another milestone on her pathway to becoming a serious detective. 'I know Pickle and I mucked up earlier, so even though we're supposed to be off the case it was only proper that we made things right. And I think you'll be quite pleased,' she added, reaching into her pinafore, 'because we've managed to get this. It's Visser's order book!' She held out the battered book, her chest still heaving from the effort of her run.

Theodore took the book in his hand and frowned. 'You really never give up, do you?' said the detective. 'But how did you get this, Wilma?' he asked, taking the book to his bureau and sitting down to examine it.

'Pickle saw that boy – Janty – with Barbu and the big man. And you said that Janty probably knew something useful. So we crept after them. Like you say all detectives should. And they went to the Lowside. And then they went into a disused building so I knew they were up to something. And I pushed over a wheel and hit the big man on the head with a pot, got the book and then we ran like mad. That's how.'

The detective considered the young girl in front of him. His eyes softened for a moment but quickly became serious. It wouldn't do for a famous and responsible detective to let a small but determined ten-year-old girl know that he was quietly impressed by her acts of foolhardy bravery. It wouldn't do at all. 'You shouldn't have done that, Wilma,' he said, leaning into the back of his chair. 'That was a very silly and dangerous thing to do.'

Wilma stared at her shoes. 'But I got the order book, didn't I?' she whispered, barely loud enough to be heard over Pickle's panting.

Theodore stood up, walked towards Wilma and stuck his thumbs into his waistcoat pockets. 'A very silly, dangerous . . . if slightly brave thing to do.'

Wilma beamed. 'But will you really be able to catch the person who ordered the fake now, Mr Goodman? I had a look, but it's like a colouring book – just full of funny pictures.'

Theodore opened the order book and examined it. 'Hmmm,' he pondered, curling the ends of his moustache between two fingers. 'It's a series of symbols and pictorial anagrams.'

'Anagrams? Is that another detective word?'

'Not really,' answered Theodore, getting out his magnifying glass again. 'It's when letters or, in this case, pictures are muddled up. And when you work out how to un-muddle them, they make a word or a sentence. Come and look.' He turned to

a random page. 'Yes – here's an easy one. So, the first column is the objects ordered. The second – by whom. What object might these refer to?'

Wilma rubbed her nose with the back of her hand and stared at the pictures. 'Looks like some sort of net. Perhaps it's something to do with a fisherman? Or a butterfly collector? Or someone who just has a lot of hair?'

'Yes, I suppose it could be, but there's also a ball going into the net. What does that tell us?'

Wilma blinked. 'That it's a ball . . . net . . . it's a ball made out of net!'

'No,' said Theodore, who was a very patient man, 'it's a goal. So that would be the first part of the clue.'

'A goal!' repeated Wilma, nodding. 'Yes, I knew that.'

'So what's this next one?' asked Theodore, pointing towards a picture of a makeshift shelter under some trees.

'Sticks and twigs!' announced Wilma. 'So we're looking for goal sticks. Made from twigs.'

'No, it's a den,' replied Theodore. 'So if we put those two clues together, what do we get?'

'A goal. And a den,' answered Wilma, scratching her head. 'Goal. And den. Goal. Den. Oh, wait! I see! Golden! Ha! Golden! Good job I'm here, Mr Goodman. To do so much contemplating and deducting!'

Theodore gave a small smile. 'So we come to our last picture. What's that?'

Wilma scrunched her face up and turned her head so she could look at the picture from a different angle. 'I think,' she said, tapping the page with some authority, 'that it's a bald-headed man. With no face.'

'No. It's an egg, Wilma,' explained Theodore, slamming Visser's order book shut. 'A golden egg! And there's only one golden egg we know of, isn't there, Wilma?'

'Is there?' answered Wilma, rubbing her chin.

'Yes!' declared Theodore. 'The Golden Egg of Polloon. One of the island's greatest treasures. You must remember it, from your Clue Ring. Case I solved a few years back.'

'Oh yes,' Wilma nodded as Pickle gave a short bark.

'Hmmm,' Theodore said, turning to the most recent orders in Visser's book. 'And this must be what we want. It's more complicated than a simple anagram. It's going to take some time to solve.' Wilma stared over the great detective's shoulder

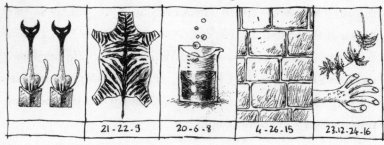

21 . 22 . 9   20 - 6 - 8   4 - 26 - 15   23.12.24.16

at the coded page in front of him.

'What does it mean, Mr Goodman?' asked Wilma.

'I'm not sure yet,' answered the detective, reaching for his notebook. 'Now then, I suspect you're hungry after your adventure. You can ask Mrs Speckle to make you some supper before you head home.'

'But . . .' began Wilma.

'No buts, young lady. Go and ask Mrs Speckle for that supper.'

'Supper?' came a sleepy voice from the chaise longue. 'Mrs Speckle?'

'Wake up, Inspector!' announced Theodore, sweeping back to his desk. 'We have the order book! Thank you, Wilma. This will really make a difference.'

Wilma was grinning from ear to ear. Even though she'd been told to go home, she had finally done something useful and not messed up. Looking up at the large round clock she realized that Mrs Waldock would probably be asleep. Maybe she could sneak in unnoticed, then go back for Mrs Waldock's picture tomorrow morning before her mistress was even up. Plus, if she was going to get her luggage tag back, now was the time. And besides, there was a mass of new evidence to add to her Clue Board! 'If you don't mind,' she said, backing out of the room, 'I won't have supper. Something I've got to do . . .' and with that she disappeared, Pickle trotting behind her.

185

'Doesn't want supper?' asked the Inspector, sitting up and rubbing his eyes. 'Has she gone QUITE mad?'

Howling Hall was as silent as a graveyard. Wilma and Pickle had crept up via the thorny bushes in the garden so that they were positioned below the blackened window of Mrs Waldock's sitting room. Wilma couldn't quite see over the top of the window ledge so she went up on her tiptoes to get a better look. Smearing the grubby glass, she rubbed a little hole in the dirt big enough to peer through. There was Mrs Waldock's chair in front of the fireplace. 'That's funny,' whispered Wilma to Pickle. 'Mrs Waldock's lit a fire. She never does that.' With the back of the chair facing her, Wilma could just make out the hand of her mistress lying motionless on the chair arm. Mrs Waldock was obviously asleep. 'Shhhh,' she whispered to Pickle. 'We need to be as quiet as mice.'

The pair tiptoed up the porch steps and in through the front door. Silently they edged their way towards the sitting room, Pickle crawling close to the floor, Wilma getting down on to her hands and knees so as not to be seen should their mistress awaken. Mrs Waldock had put the luggage tag in the front pocket of her cardigan, and as Wilma inched her way forward she could see it was still in there wedged between the chair and Mrs Waldock's arm. Gingerly Wilma reached up until she found

the tag's knotted string. Sweat had broken out on Wilma's brow, and Pickle's forehead was furrowed with anxiety. The room was warm from the fire, and as Wilma tugged on the tag she was worried that her sweaty fingers would slip. Slowly it came towards her, but its end was stuck. Screwing her eyes closed and biting her bottom lip, Wilma took the plunge and pulled. Mrs Waldock's body shifted and suddenly her resting arm came thumping down to hit Wilma on the face. Wilma let out a small squeal, but something wasn't right. Mrs Waldock showed no signs of waking. The disturbed arm hung limp and lifeless, inches from Wilma's nose. Wilma stood up and peered more closely at her mistress. She waved a hand in front of her eyes . . . nothing. She put an ear to her mouth . . . no sign of breathing. Wilma stood back and stared. It couldn't be? But as Wilma reached forward and placed a hand on Mrs Waldock's chest, she made her biggest deduction to date.

Mrs Waldock was dead. And her heart was frozen. How utterly horrid.

CHAPTER 22

'Is it too much to ask . . .' screamed Barbu D'Anvers, as he was pulled out from under the milling wheel, 'that for once, I am not surrounded by incompetence and stupidity?'

Tully shifted on his feet and rubbed the back of his head. 'The thing is,' he began, with a gulp, 'is that I didn't see her coming, and what with the pot and the dog and everything I just—'

'Tully!' snapped Barbu, clenching his fists. 'She's a little girl. A little GIRL! I'm so sorry, but I was under the impression that I pay you to be my thuggish sidekick. I don't think it's unreasonable to expect that you could cope with fighting off a small, badly dressed child and her stinking hound.' Tully bit his lip. 'We had the order book in our grasp!' continued Barbu, throwing a brick at the henchman. 'And it's gone! How am I going to find the Katzin Stone now?'

'I thought you needed the order book to organize a tribute

188

for my father? And find his killer?' said Janty, who was standing in the corner, having dusted himself down.

'Rule number one of being evil,' snapped Barbu. 'Never tell the truth! Of course I wasn't organizing a tribute! I want to find the Katzin Stone! And now that ghastly girl has the order book, it's only a matter of time before Theodore P. Goody-Two-Shoes is hot on the jewel's tail! We have to do something! Think, boy! You worked with your father! You must have seen something!'

A small flash of anger sparked in Janty's eyes. He had been tricked by Barbu, but he knew that the villain was also his only hope of revenge. It was suddenly clear: help him find the stone and he might catch his father's killer too. 'I want to be bad. Like you,' he said defiantly. 'Will you teach me everything? Like my father was teaching me? If you will, then I will help you. If you won't, you get nothing from me.'

Barbu D'Anvers was momentarily speechless. He had been planning on killing the boy once he was no longer useful, so this was a development he wasn't ready for. His eyes widened a little. 'Well, well,' he said eventually. 'How very bold. Bargaining with *me*? You're taking a grave risk. Although I have to admit I'm impressed. It shows ambition. And is the sort of dirty trick I admire. You want to be bad?' he added, with a twirl of his cane. 'I suppose it depends how bad you want to be. I don't know if you've got it in you.'

'I have, Mr D'Anvers,' urged Janty, his grey eyes flashing. 'I don't ever want to be good. Not as long as I live.'

'Well,' said Barbu, 'let's start with thinking about that stone, shall we? And then I'll whip up something basic for you to do to begin with, like . . . poking someone with a stick. You can probably manage that.'

'Yes, Mr D'Anvers,' nodded Janty. 'Then let's shake on it. From now on you will be my master.' He thrust his grubby hand towards Barbu.

Barbu smiled. 'Hmmm,' he grinned, taking Janty's hand in his. 'I do like the sound of that. All right, you have a bargain. We shall shake.'

And as Janty sealed his fate, the last light of the day sank away into blackness.

Now that the boy had made his decision, he was lost in thought. *Did* he know anything? His father had always been careful not to allow him to his secret meetings, despite Janty's protestations. It was for his own safety, Visser had insisted, but he had seen the Katzin Stone being made – the client had paid extra to have the work completed in double-quick time. Janty's father had worked day and night on it for two days. 'I think,' Janty began, his eyebrows knitted in concentration, 'my father did mention it might be a particularly high-profile case – sometimes those clients asked him to hide the original once it was obtained in one of our famed secret deposit boxes. You know, until the heat died down, even to sell it on for them . . .'

'What?' hissed Barbu, his eyes widening. 'The real Katzin Stone could be hidden somewhere where we can find it?'

'Well, it might be,' said Janty, with a shrug. 'If my father hid it, then I can probably work out where. He had several hiding places dotted round the island.'

Barbu shoved Tully to one side and leaned forward to grip his young charge's shoulder. Bending down so that his nose was almost touching Janty's, and fixing him with a penetrating stare, Barbu hissed, 'Find it for me. Find it for me *now*.'

It was late. After many hours of searching, it was dark, they were cold and Barbu, not famed for his patience, was at the end of his tether. They had already been to seven locations on the island, including the back of the pigsties at Whiffling Farm, the thorny bush on the edge of Dunderhead Gorge and the cistern in the second toilet on the left at Mr Hankley's Corn Crumble Factory. Everywhere Janty had taken them had turned up nothing.

'How many hiding places can one man have?' Barbu yelled, as Tully helped him pull one of his legs out of a particularly sticky pool of mud. 'What's wrong with something simple? Like an iron box with a key? Or a very deep pocket? Nothing! Look at my boots! The suede is ruined!'

'Just one more place, Mr D'Anvers,' said Janty, trudging ahead of his master, lantern aloft. A mist had rolled in from the sea and was so thick the light from the burning candle barely penetrated it. 'There's a potting shed on the Lowside allotments. If my father hid the Katzin Stone, that's our last hope.'

'It'll be your last hope if it's not there,' spat Barbu, poking his young charge in the back. 'Well, let's get on with it. The sooner we end this ridiculous farce the better!'

The Lowside allotments were shrouded in a dense fog, giving the ivy-covered canes a sinister appearance. The potting shed that Janty's father had used as a hiding point was towards the back. 'There it is,' mumbled Janty, gesturing with his lantern.

'Break the door,' ordered Barbu with a low growl, pointing towards a padlock hanging on a loop of metal over the handle. 'Do it now.'

Tully stepped forward, his breath billowing in the cold night air. Taking a large iron wrench from his pocket he smashed down on the padlock, sending it broken to the floor. He pulled open the door and Barbu entered, his cloak wrapped tight about him.

The shed was a tip. Tools, pots and papers scattered the floor. Barbu, wild-eyed, gave Tully and Janty a shove and shouted, 'Well, go on, start searching!' Tully, eager to put his shameful defeat at the hands of a ten-year-old behind him, started

opening drawers and emptying everything he could get his hands on. Pencils, pots of paint, seed packets, old keys, twine and a broken teapot spout tumbled about his feet. Janty, in contrast, stood very still and looked about him. 'Where is it?' yelled Barbu, banging his cane on the floor. 'Where did he put it?'

'Wait!' shouted Janty. 'My father always said, "If you want to hide something, put it in plain view."'

Barbu's head snapped round, his eyes narrowing as he scanned the cramped space. 'There!' he said, with a quiet air of excitement. 'Look at the head of that watering can. Shine the lantern on it, Janty.'

Everyone's gaze followed Barbu's pointing finger. Just above a shelf of seeding trays there was a squat green watering can. Janty held up the lantern and there, in the light, something twinkled on the spout's head. Barbu stepped over the mess on the floor and tried to grab at it. 'Hmmm . . . can't quite . . .'

'Shall I get you a stool to stand on?' asked Tully, looking for something suitable. 'You know, so you can reach?'

Barbu spun back round. 'Tully,' he began, his face contorted with anger, 'I am perfectly capable of reaching anything and everything. But on this occasion I can't be bothered, so why don't you get it down instead? Seeing as that's your JOB!'

The henchman bumbled forward and lifted down the watering can. 'Here you are, Mr Barbu,' he mumbled, passing it down

to his tiny master. Barbu, who was still glaring, snatched the can. 'Aha!' he declared. 'I think we have what we've been looking for!' For instead of a watering-can rose on the end of the spout, the sparkling splendour of the Katzin Stone was wedged there. Barbu, taking it in his hand and holding it up into the lantern light, threw back his head and let out a triumphant laugh. 'It's mine!' he guffawed. 'I stole it right from under their noses! I'm rich beyond my wildest dreams! The island is mine!' Barbu tossed the stone into the air, watched it as it dazzled, caught it and slipped it into his breast coat pocket.

'But our work is not yet done,' he added, his smile turning to a scowl. 'Someone tried to outwit me. And I don't like it. There is only one arch-villain on Cooper! And it's me! Before we celebrate, we're going to track down the man behind this and kill him! Aren't we, Janty?'

'But we don't know who he is,' said Tully, looking a bit puzzled. 'We haven't got the book.'

Barbu's top lip curled. 'Yes, Tully,' he snarled, 'I know we haven't got the book. And whose fault is that? Nonetheless, there must be other ways of working it out. Now think, both of you. What else do we know? Anything?'

'I read that the man who found the stone and his aunt, the ones who were killed, both had some lavender in their hands,' said Janty, looking hopeful. 'I don't know if that means anything.'

194

'Wait!' said Barbu, thinking hard. 'Lavender? Someone tried to give me . . . well, well . . . I'm an obvious target. Whoever it is wants to be the greatest villain on Cooper, and only I can prevent that. The lady at the Tweve Rats' Tails! I was right. No man would dare to out-manoeuvre me on this island. But a woman is a different matter. We are looking for a woman! Think you can manage that, Tully?'

Tully scowled but nodded. He'd been beaten by one female and he wasn't about to let it happen again. Whoever she was, her days were numbered. He would make sure of it.

CHAPTER 23

'Lavender,' said Theodore, opening the hand of the very dead Mrs Waldock. 'As I suspected.'

'And I'll wager her heart is frozen too, Goodman,' weighed in the Inspector, wiping his brow with his handkerchief. 'Just like the others. I don't like it. Don't like it one bit.'

'Come here, Wilma,' said the detective softly, looking into a darkened corner of the room. Wilma, still shocked from her discovery, edged forward, her head hanging low. 'Now, can you tell me anything? Anything that you noticed when you came in? Was there anything unusual or out of the ordinary?'

Wilma clutched her luggage tag to her chest. 'I can't think of anything, Mr Goodman. I just thought she was asleep . . .' Her voice trailed off and she shivered a little. Pickle gave himself a sympathetic shake. 'Although, hang on . . .' Wilma's eyes brightened. 'The fire!' she declared, pointing in its direction.

'Mrs Waldock never made up the fire! Even on a cold night. She always said it was a waste of coal. So that was different.'

'Hmmm,' said Theodore, walking over to the hearth and looking into it. He picked up a small iron poker that was hanging on a hook and poked at the still-hot coals.

'Perhaps the villain needed to burn something, Mr Goodman,' suggested Wilma. 'Destroy evidence? Like when Barbu D'Anvers burned all those cloth caps when you solved the Case of the Three-Stringed Ukelele?'

'Perhaps,' said the detective, frowning a little. 'Or perhaps not.' He turned and stared at the body slumped in the chair. 'We'll let Dr Kooks and Penbert take over from here on. Although I suspect they'll just confirm what I now know.'

'And what's that?' asked Wilma, trying to look as if she already had an inkling, which, of course, she didn't.

'Not yet, Wilma,' said Theodore, tapping the magnifying glass in his waistcoat pocket. 'Top tip number eight, remember? Proper detectives always save what they're thinking till last. Hang on a minute. What's this?' The great detective leaned towards the body and peered at the shoulder. Taking a pair of tweezers from his top breast pocket, he carefully lifted off something small, bright and shiny. 'Well, I never,' he said, holding it up to the light. 'A false fingernail.'

'That's odd,' said Wilma, making a mental note to add it to

her Clue Board. 'Although Mrs Waldock got me to chew her fingernails right down, so maybe she got herself some nice ones. To stick on.'

'Interesting,' Theodore mumbled, dropping the blood-red fingernail into a bag and handing it to the Inspector. 'Did anyone visit Mrs Waldock earlier, Wilma? Anyone at all?'

Wilma shook her head. 'Mrs Waldock didn't seem like she ever had visitors. In fact, she never left the house while I was there. The only person I ever heard her speak about was that man in the photo Pickle broke. I don't know who he was though.'

'Have you got that photo?' asked Theodore. 'Can you show it to me?'

'No,' answered Wilma. 'It's still at Miss DeChrista's Framing Emporium. I left it there yesterday when I followed Janty and the others. But hang on . . .' she added, remembering. 'There's other stuff! Upstairs in a costume trunk!'

'Costume trunk?' asked Inspector Lemone, scratching his forehead. 'What would Mrs Waldock be doing with a costume trunk?'

'Fetch it for me, please, Wilma,' said the great detective, getting out his pipe. 'It may be nothing but we shouldn't overlook it.'

Wilma scampered to fetch the trunk's most interesting con-

tents, eager as always to show Mr Goodman that she was worthy of being a detective's apprentice. With Mrs Waldock dead, her future on the Farside was uncertain but not hopeless.

'Here you are, Mr Goodman,' puffed Wilma, returning. 'I brought down this poster. It looks like she belonged to a circus or something.'

Theodore peered at the picture. 'Perhaps you could look into that, Lemone? Find out whether the circus is still around – if anyone remembers Mrs Waldock or her gentleman friend.'

'Will do,' said the Inspector with a nod.

'Well,' declared Theodore, packing his pipe with some rosemary tobacco, 'nothing more we can do here. I think you should be getting to bed, Wilma. It's been a long day. Gather your things. We'll ask Mrs Speckle to make up the spare room until we can work out what to do with you,' he added. 'Can't have you staying here, not now Mrs Waldock is gone.'

Wilma had never had anyone really care for her apart from Pickle, and as Theodore and the Inspector walked with her to the front door a gentle warm glow radiated through her chest. Here she was with the famous and serious Theodore P. Goodman, about to stay with him in his house and sit drinking peppermint tea and eating biscuits just like a proper detective. Bit by bit she was creeping towards her dream, and one day, she

thought, she wouldn't be trying to work out why her horrible ex-employer was lying dead in an armchair, she'd be finding out what was meant by that mysterious luggage tag left about her wrist when she was a baby. She looked down at her Clue Board on top of her bundle of things – she'd already started to update it while Mr Goodman and the Inspector had been finishing off in Mrs Waldock's living room. Surely there were some answers on it by now . . .

They had just reached the broken gate of Howling Hall when they heard a cart approaching. It was a black buggy drawn by two black horses, and as it made an abrupt stop a cloud of dust was kicked up into Wilma's face. She squinted her eyes and coughed.

'Wilma Tenderfoot?' said a voice that sounded like knives being sharpened. Out from the dust loomed a face that Wilma knew all too well. It was Madam Skratch. 'Well, this is an inconvenience, I must say,' she barked, her pointed nose bobbing up and down. 'I received the telegram a couple of hours ago. Mrs Waldock dead? I hope you had nothing to do with it.'

'No . . . I . . .' Wilma began.

'Telegram?' asked Theodore, stepping forward. 'What telegram?'

'Don't be ridiculous,' snapped the matron. 'What telegram indeed? The telegram YOU sent me, Mr Goodman. In fact, here

it is!' She reached into her overcoat and pulled out a small yellow piece of paper.

Theodore reached up and read it. 'Barbara Waldock dead. Wilma Tenderfoot to be returned to Institute immediately. Theodore P. Goodman.' The great detective looked back up. 'But I never sent this telegram. It must have been sent by the killer!'

'Why does the killer want me back at the Institute?' wailed Wilma, clutching the ends of her pinafore.

'I'll thank you not to speak,' boomed the matron, holding out a hand. 'I have absolutely no interest in anything you might have to say. So let's get this over with. Into the cart, please. You're going back to the Institute.'

'What?' wailed Wilma. 'No! But I can't! I . . .'

'Surely Wilma doesn't have to go back quite yet?' Theodore stepped in as Madam Skratch clutched Wilma's shoulder with her bony fingers. 'The girl has had a terrible shock! Are you sure this is necessary? I did not send that telegram, Madam Skratch!'

'I couldn't care less who sent it. And yes, I'm afraid it's very necessary,' snapped back Madam Skratch, dragging Wilma towards the buggy. 'Orphans make me money! It's quite plain. It's in the small print.' Tossing Wilma up in to the back of the buggy, Madam Skratch reached again into the dark folds of her corseted dress and pulled out a contract. 'Here!' she added, waving it in Theodore's direction. 'At the bottom. In the event of the

employer's death, the child will return to being the property of the Institute to do with as they think fit. She's mine, more's the pity. Goodnight!'

As Madam Skratch turned to get back into the buggy, Pickle bounced forward and put his paws on the side plate to jump up next to Wilma. 'Get down!' yelled Madam Skratch, giving him a kick with her boot. 'Filthy creature!'

'But that's my dog!' cried Wilma, whose face was now streaming with tears. 'Please let me take my dog!'

'No dogs allowed!' hissed the cruel matron with a sneer. 'As you well know. Thank you, driver! Return us to the Institute immediately!'

'This is monstrous!' cried out Inspector Lemone, whose cheeks had turned a livid scarlet. 'You can't treat a child like a spare wheel!'

As the buggy turned about and the driver raised his whip to speed off, Theodore P. Goodman leaped forward and pressed something into Wilma's hand. 'The Case of the Broken Spindle, Wilma,' he urged, eyes wide and earnest. 'Don't forget! Just push it through! Push it through!'

'What?' said Wilma, gulping back tears.

But it was too late for Theodore to answer. With a loud and agitated whinny, the horses galloped off and Wilma could only watch in desperation as her three friends along with all

202

her detective hopes and her dreams of finding her own family disappeared into the distance just as she was starting to get somewhere. Wiping at her eyes, she opened her hand to see what her hero had given her. In her palm there was a piece of string, a safety pin and a matchstick. 'Push it through?' she mumbled. 'Push what through where?'

CHAPTER 24

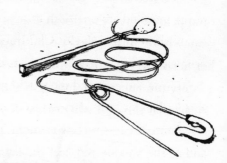

The Lowside Institute for Woeful Children was even more grim and desolate than Wilma remembered. Shrouded in a mist, its skinny turrets piercing the gloom, the Institute looked foreboding and joyless. Wilma felt the cold chill of misery engulf her. Before she had left the Institute she had managed to accept her lot and plod along happily enough, but now that she had had a proper opportunity to pursue detecting and, more importantly, had felt the warmth that friendship could offer, her return was as desperate an experience as she could recollect.

'Come with me, Tenderfoot,' growled Madam Skratch as the buggy drew up in front of the Institute's entrance. Taking Wilma by her collar, Madam Skratch marched through the dark and hostile corridors, the only noise the sound of the matron's boot heels clipping the stone floors as they went, the only decoration an enormous tapestry of the Institute's motto: 'Things might

get better, but they probably won't' which – to be honest, had never instilled anyone with much confidence, but then it was an establishment for Woeful Children and, as such, there was little point in raising anyone's expectations.

Wilma had assumed she would go to the dormitory and so was shocked and a little alarmed to discover that she was being taken down into the Institute's basement. The air smelled damp and dirty and as she was shoved past the laundry room she stumbled over heaps of mouldy socks and rancid pants. At the end of the narrow corridor there was a heavy metal door that sat unevenly on the stone floor beneath it. A large iron key was in its lock. Madam Skratch heaved the door open and waved the key in Wilma's face. 'You will stay in here until I decide otherwise,' she barked, pushing Wilma into the cell-like room. 'You can use your time to contemplate your useless existence.' And with that, the door was slammed shut and all Wilma was left with was the sound of a key turning and sharp footsteps clicking away into the distance.

Well. This was a fine mess. A stolen stone and four murders to solve and here was Wilma stuck in a stinking room with no hope of being any help to anyone. She looked around. There was a small window in the wall to her left which, if she stood on the tips of her toes, she could just see out of. She stared across the Institute's front yard towards a scrub of trees just beyond the high iron fence. A wind was blowing and the treetops were swaying in the moonlight. Wilma pushed at the window, but it was stuck tight. If there was a way out, that wasn't it. Dropping back down to the floor, Wilma headed for the meagre bed in the corner of the room and sat down heavily on it with her face cradled in her cupped hands. 'Ouch!' she said, reaching underneath her pinafore and pulling out a long, hard length of straw that was poking up painfully from the mattress. She threw it on to the floor and heaved a sigh. She had been so close to achieving her dream. She felt certain that, with Mrs Waldock gone, it would only have been a matter of time before the detective had asked her to be his apprentice. And with the proper training she would have been closer than ever to discovering the truth behind her past. But Madam Skratch had ruined all that. Wilma hadn't done enough. Theodore P. Goodman had let her go.

Outside the wind was picking up, and as Wilma kicked at the stony floor with frustration she could hear the soft howling of it in the trees. She looked sadly at her worn luggage tag and creased Clue Board. She sighed again. 'Pickle . . .' she whispered with longing, but the thought of her best friend was too much to bear and Wilma lay her head into the crook of her elbow and at last gave way to tears. Then, having resigned herself to life back at the Institute, she drifted into a miserable sleep.

As Wilma lay sleeping the howls of the wind seemed to rise in step with her own melancholic dreams, but then there

began to be something familiar about the sound, something more tangible than just wind whipping through the treetops. Wilma forced herself awake to see the first light of dawn streaming in through the window. She rubbed her eyes roughly with the back of her pinafore and sat up so as to listen better. There it was again, a deeper sound that she couldn't quite place. It stopped, and for a moment Wilma thought she'd imagined it. But then it came again! A baying yowl that cut through the wind! She knew that noise! Wilma rushed to the window and pulled herself upwards. 'Pickle!' she shouted, half laughing, half crying. And there he was, sitting obediently just beyond the iron fence calling out for Wilma. She couldn't believe her eyes. 'He must have run all the way!' she spluttered.

Wilma banged on the window with her fist. 'Pickle! I'm here!' The beagle's head was stretched upwards in mid-howl, but as he heard his name his ears pricked and his head snapped suddenly in the direction of the low window in the wall ahead of him. Wilma banged again on the windowpane and waved her hand wildly. Pickle let out an excited yelp, spun on the spot and gave three barks for good measure. Wilma laughed. Seeing her loyal beagle filled her with determination. Somehow she had to escape. Theodore P. Goodman would never give up and neither would she! But how could she get out?

She turned away from the window and stuck both her hands

into the front of her pinafore. And then she felt them, the matchstick, string and safety pin that Detective Goodman had given her. How could she have forgotten? Pulling them out of her pocket she stared down at the objects in her hand. What was it he had said to her? 'Push it through, Wilma,' she muttered to herself, a small frown spreading across her forehead. 'And what was the other thing? Something about a case? The Case of the Broken Spindle? Wait a minute!' she suddenly declared, eyes widening. 'It's on my Clue Ring!'

Grabbing for the bundle of clippings on her belt, she fell to her knees and flicked through, opening every piece of paper that she had. 'Here it is!' she squealed as she unfolded a particularly old clipping. 'The Case of the Broken Spindle!' she read, scanning the page as fast as she could. 'Locked in a room . . . seemed impossible . . . all he had was a matchstick, a piece of string and a safety pin!' Wilma grabbed the three items and ran to the locked door. 'He used the matchstick to push the key so it fell to the floor on the other side! He's telling me to escape!'

Her hand shaking with excitement, Wilma poked the matchstick into the keyhole. 'Oh no,' she said, crestfallen. 'It's too short! Now what am I going to do? I need something longer!' Wilma spun about, her eyes searching wildly. 'The straw!' she yelled, dashing forward to pick up the particularly tough bit of straw that had made her bed so uncomfortable earlier. Running

back to the keyhole, she pushed the stalk of the straw inwards until she could feel it come up against the key. Slowly and firmly she applied pressure, wiggling the straw a little until, with one tiny click, she heard the key settle itself free. Holding her end of the straw, Wilma gave a sharp shove and to her relief she felt the key shoot out of the keyhole and fall to the floor outside her cell. It had worked! Wilma got down on her hands and knees and peered through the gap. She could see the key! But how could she get it? Quickly she looked back at the newspaper clipping. 'He tied a safety pin to a piece of string, opened the safety pin out and then, throwing it under the door, used it as a hook to pull the key towards him! Brilliant! It's brilliant!' Wilma followed the instructions to the letter and flicked the homemade fishing rod through the gap under the door. Sliding the string sideways, she positioned the safety pin and slowly, very slowly, pulled it towards the key. It took a few goes but finally, at the fifth attempt, the sharp end of the safety pin caught itself under the key. Carefully Wilma drew in the string. The key was moving towards her! It was working! One more tug and the key was in the gap under the door. Wilma reached with her fingers and the key was hers!

She stood up, triumphant. 'I'm coming, Pickle!' she shouted. 'Nobody and nothing stops Wilma Tenderfoot!' And as she unlocked the door and ran off down the dark, dank corridor, there was no reason to believe otherwise.

CHAPTER 25

'Inspector!' shouted Theodore, waving at his portly friend, who was sweating as he paced towards him. 'As fast as you can! We're late for the Curator! Then we need to get on and visit that Cynta tree – look for further clues. Did you find anything?'

'Certainly did,' puffed Inspector Lemone, handing the world-famous detective a file as they walked. 'It seems that in her younger years Mrs Waldock used to be an illusionist's glamorous assistant at Grimbles's Circus. Even better, the owner's still alive – we're tracking her down to ask her more about Mrs Waldock's possible fella.'

'Interesting,' said Goodman, eyebrows raised. 'Good work, Lemone!'

'I say, Goodman,' panted the Inspector as he trotted to keep up, 'couldn't we just have sent the Curator a note? Did we really

need to come to the Museum? I've barely finished my breakfast.'

'Meetings are not just for the client's benefit, Lemone!' Theodore declared, reaching to open the door in front of them. 'Aah, Mr Curator and Miss Pagne!' he beamed. 'Sorry we're a little late. The Inspector was running an errand for me.'

'That girl's not with you?' asked Miss Pagne, arching to see over the detective's shoulder. She was sitting at a small desk where she was playing a game of Patience with great finesse. Her hair was loose about her shoulders and she was wearing an orange fitted jacket with an elaborate diamond snake pin running through the lapel.

'No,' replied Theodore, shaking his head. 'I'm afraid she was taken back to the Institute last night – what with her mistress having been killed.'

'Seems a terrible shame,' muttered the Curator, placing his cane into a side cupboard.

'That's an interesting pair of scissors,' commented Inspector Lemone, pointing towards Miss Pagne's desk suddenly. 'They for something special?'

'They're specialist trimming shears,' answered Miss Pagne, pushing a dark curl out of her eyes. 'For bonsai trees. I have a weakness for them – as you can see.'

The glamorous assistant gestured with a painted fingernail to a group of three plinths behind the Inspector. On top of each

was a miniature, intricately pruned tree. Miss Pagne slunk over to the one nearest her and made a small snip, sending a little wayward branch tumbling to the floor.

'Keen on plants, are you?' asked the Inspector as he watched it fall.

Miss Pagne shrugged elegantly. 'I'm interested in all beautiful things, Inspector. Like you, Mr Goodman,' she added, looking at Theodore through lowered lashes. 'You enjoy the finer things in life, I'm sure.' The detective met her gaze and held it.

'That will do, Miss Pagne,' grumbled the Curator.

The Inspector's eyes narrowed. 'I say, ever seen a Cynta tree?'

Miss Pagne turned her head away and moved to the second bonsai. 'I have heard of it, of course. But I've never seen one.'

'Cynta tree?' coughed the Curator. 'Why? What's that?'

'Well . . .' began the Inspector, clearing his throat a little.

But Theodore interrupted him. 'That's not actually why we're here.' The great detective reached into the depths of his overcoat and pulled out the battered leather order book. 'It belonged to the forger,' he explained, handing it to the Curator. 'All his orders are listed. And his clients. But it is in code.'

'Have you managed to crack it?' said the Curator, thumbing quickly through the book's pages.

'Not yet, no,' answered Theodore.

'How did you get it?' asked the Curator.

'Wilma stole it right from Barbu D'Anvers himself,' puffed Inspector Lemone.

'If I was him, I'd probably want her dead,' mused Miss Pagne, looking sideways at the order book.

'But she's safely locked up at the Institute now,' added the Curator, 'so I don't expect she'll be causing any more trouble.'

'Oh, don't count on it!' beamed Inspector Lemone. 'Theodore's given her everything she needs to escape! That girl is so determined, she'll get out and probably have the villain before we do! Ha ha!' He narrowed his eyes deliberately in Miss Pagne's direction as he spoke.

Theodore's jaw tightened and he put a hand on his friend's arm to stop him. 'That's enough, Inspector,' he said, in a near whisper. 'I'm sure the Curator isn't interested in a ten-year-old girl.'

'Yes, well,' said the Curator standing at his desk. 'I have things to attend to. Let me know when you get somewhere with that book, won't you, Goodman? Miss Pagne, I wonder if you could run this note over to the Ministry?'

'No need for a note,' answered Miss Pagne, taking the letter. 'I'll send a telegram. Always quicker.' Pulling on a large dark shawl, she turned and nodded in the detective's direction. 'Mr Goodman, always a pleasure.' And with that she slipped away.

'I say, Goodman,' mumbled the Inspector, giving his friend a nudge, 'you don't think that—'

'Not now, Inspector, the Curator wants to get on,' said Theodore with some urgency. 'And so do we. Mr Curator, thank you for seeing us.'

'But . . .' spluttered the Inspector as he was bundled out of the room. Theodore closed the door behind them and raised a finger to his lips. 'Don't you think it was suspicious though?' the Inspector went on, donning his hat and following the detective as he strode away down the corridor. 'Miss Pagne knowing about trees and telegrams? Red nails. Seemed quite rattled too.'

'Things are starting to come together,' said Theodore, stabbing a finger into the air. 'Do you still have Mrs Waldock's lavender?'

'Got it in my pocket, Goodman,' said the Inspector, reaching to pull it out. 'Bagged up obviously. Proper procedure and all that. Haven't had a chance to send it to the lab yet.'

But the detective had his notebook out and was scribbling fiercely. He didn't look up as Lemone lifted the bag to his face. 'Still. Odd that she was killed. Can't see what she had to do with the case,' the Inspector went on. 'Love the smell of lavender,' he added absent-mindedly and, pulling the top of the bag open, he took one, deep sniff.

Theodore, who had his back to the Inspector, was now twiddling his moustache in his fingers, lost in thought. 'Hmmm,' he pondered, 'it is odd that Mrs Waldock was added to the chain of

victims. All her death has succeeded in doing is sending Wilma back to the Institute. Unless . . .' His eyes widened. 'I have a terrible feeling,' he said in his most serious tone to date, 'that Wilma is in grave danger.'

'Wilma . . .' answered Inspector Lemone, in a lazy, slurred voice, 'danger . . . I . . .'

Theodore turned round sharply just as his friend, eyes rolling to the back of his head, slumped to the floor. The detective heaved Lemone into his arms. Taking the opened lavender bag from the Inspector's hand, Theodore raised it causiously to his nose, but flinched and threw it down again almost straightaway. 'As I thought,' he muttered. 'Chloroform! The killer used lavender infused with chloroform to drug the victims before killing them!' Above his head, on a table, there was a small vase with some flowers in. Theodore reached up and, taking the flowers out, threw the water into Inspector Lemone's face.

'What the . . . ?' spluttered the Inspector, coming round. 'I say . . . no need for . . . What were you saying about Wilma?'

'She's in the gravest danger, Inspector. We haven't a moment to lose.'

'But she's at that wretched Institute,' said Lemone, stumbling to his feet.

'By now she may not be,' answered Theodore, racing to the

door. 'I should never have given her the means to escape! We have to find her. And hope that *we* get to her first.'

The Inspector blinked. 'Then wait for me, Goodman!' he shouted. And for the first time in ten years, he ran as quickly as his legs would carry him.

CHAPTER 26

W ilma was heading for the kitchen. If she could get through there unseen, then she could leave by the small side door that led out to the bins at the back of the Institute. From there she could climb over the scraps heap, on to the brick wall that rounded the enclosure and hop from there on to the potato patch that led, in turn, to the gap in the iron fence through which, if she held her breath and hoped for the best, she could squeeze and escape.

It was just before lunch, when everyone at the Institute would be in the Pit, carrying lumps of coal for no discernible reason, but all the same she needed to be careful. Wilma eased the kitchen door open and crept through, mindful not to make a sound. Halfway through, she heard a click of heels behind her. Every muscle in Wilma's body stiffened. Madam Skratch was in the pantry. There was nowhere to hide. What was Wilma going to do?

*

Madam Skratch had decided that she was going to have more onions than usual in her pudding that lunchtime, mostly because she was scheduled to punish a nine-year-old boy called Franklin Muslette that afternoon and she wanted to breathe on him in an odious manner. As she piled the sliced onions on top of her trifle she suddenly stopped, looked up and frowned. Had she heard something? Was someone in the kitchen? She put down the knife and popped her head out of the pantry door. 'Is anybody here?' she barked, scanning the room. No answer. Madam Skratch's eyes tightened into slits. She had heard something, and if there was one thing she was sure of, it was that Woeful Children liked to steal food. Very slowly she bent down and looked under the butcher's block. Nothing. 'There's a child in here,' she announced loudly. 'I can sense it. So it would be better for you if you came out now. Or there will be serious consequences!'

A heavy silence filled the room. Madam Skratch pursed her lips, her eyes darting left and right for the slightest sign of movement. And then she saw it. Over in the corner, by the barrel of sun-dried Brussels sprouts, were the hooks where the chefs hung their aprons. One apron looked peculiarly lumpy. 'Aha,' whispered the mean-spirited matron. 'Now I have you.' Treading quietly, she tiptoed, skinny hand outstretched, and then, when it was within her grasp, she reached forward and snatched the

apron off its hook! The mop that was leaning inside fell to the floor. Madam Skratch stared at it, a little disappointed. Then, taking one last look about her, she returned to the pantry, where she took a large, greedy spoonful of her onion-packed trifle.

The apron to the left of the one Madam Skratch had snatched twitched and rustled into life. Wilma, who had been holding her breath in terror lest she be caught, heaved a sigh of relief and quickly slipped from her hiding place and out the back door. Clambering over the heap of vegetable peelings and scraps of unwanted gristle, she pulled herself up on to the wall that divided the kitchen quarters from the potato patch and jumped down. Not daring to look back, she sprinted through the plants, leaves whipping at her knees, to the place in the iron fence where she knew there was the slimmest of gaps. Pickle, who had seen her running across the garden, had scampered to meet her and was letting out small, excited yelps. Wilma squeezed herself through with a wriggle and Pickle, beside himself with joy, leaped into her arms and licked her face with enthusiasm.

'Yuck!' laughed Wilma, wiping the dog slobber from her cheeks. 'I'm pleased to see you too! But we can't stay here. It's too dangerous. We've got to find Mr Goodman. Let's try and work out where he'll be.' Wilma reached into her pinafore pocket and pulled out her crumpled Clue Board. 'So it started with the stone in the vault. Then Alan Katzin and his aunt were killed. Then the stone dissolved in the box. (That was the fake one. We know that. The real one was swapped using some kind of magic hands.) Then the man who made the fake was also killed. By a dart that you found, Pickle. Well done. But then you ate it. Not so well done for that. Anyway, the dart came from the air vent, which I think is important. Then I got the order book, which was a load of anagrams. Then Mrs Waldock was killed. And there was the poster. In the costume trunk. And there was lavender. And the fish scale. And the fingernail. And loads of hearts being frozen. We mustn't forget that.'

Wilma stopped and gave a sigh of concentration. Tapping the pencil against her lips, she stared at the pictures she had drawn. Pickle lifted up his paw and put it on the updated Clue Board. 'The air vent?' asked Wilma. 'Is that what you're pointing at?' Pickle flapped his ears. 'I think you're right. It's a large clue that hasn't been investigated. And Mr Goodman did say that if he could work out who killed Visser then the case would be solved! That's it! I bet they've gone there! And even if they haven't – we should! That way we can help Mr Goodman make his final deductions! I know he said I shouldn't rush about searching for clues and following him, but I don't work for Mrs Waldock any more, and if I find the clue that helps Mr Goodman finally solve the case then he absolutely, positively will have to have me as his apprentice! And although he said the air vent might not be that

helpful a clue, that's probably just because he and the Inspector are too big to climb through it – that's probably why he wanted me to escape, so I could check it out. There's a cart that leaves the Institute just after lunch to take letters and parcels, so if we creep on to the back of that we'll be able to get there even faster. Oh, Pickle!' she added, throwing her arms around the tatty-eared beagle. 'I love you so much!'

But as the plucky pair jumped onto the backboard of the postal cart and crawled under the tarpaulin they had no way of knowing that they were closer to Theodore than they thought. Because the detective and a very sweaty Inspector Lemone were coming the other way on their tandem. And as Theodore banged on the front door of the Institute, Wilma and Pickle were being driven towards nothing but a very untimely end.

Oh dear. Don't stop reading now. It's about to get worse.

CHAPTER 27

'There's no one here,' whispered Wilma, poking her head into Visser's workshop late that afternoon. 'Be careful, Pickle, there are things broken everywhere.'

Wilma picked her way across the room through the debris to the air vent. Climbing on to a stool and reaching with one hand, she slid the cover up and peered into the pitch-black tube. 'I need to be able to see,' she called down to Pickle. 'Can you find a candle or anything?'

Pickle looked around the room. The floor was covered with the scattered contents of drawers and boxes. With his nose to the floor he got busy, found something, picked it up and trotted back to Wilma. 'No,' said Wilma, 'that's a sock, Pickle. Socks don't really work as torches. Hang on. I'll come down and help.'

Jumping off the stool, Wilma got on to her hands and knees and rummaged through the rubbish on the floor. 'People

always keep candles in drawers,' she explained to Pickle, who now had the stinking sock between his front paws and was chewing it. 'In case of emergencies. And this is an emergency so we just need to find one. Aha!' Triumphant, Wilma held up a stubby, half-candle. 'I've still got the matchstick Mr Goodman gave me,' Wilma added, reaching into her pinafore pocket. There was a rough edge on the tipped-over workbench to her right. She struck the matchstick against it and it fizzed into life. With the candle lit, she waded her way back over to the air vent.

'Pickle,' she said, turning to look at her beagle, 'you can't come with me. It's too tricky for dogs. So I'm going to write a note and you're going to take it to Mr Goodman. He'll want to meet me and do some deducting. You know, when I'm back with loads of clues.' Wilma scribbled as she spoke, tore the page from her notebook and bent down to stuff the note under Pickle's collar. 'There. Go find Mr Goodman, Pickle! Take him the note!'

The call of destiny comes eventually to all small hounds with a noble heart, and as Pickle heard and understood the great detective's name and saw his beloved friend going into battle alone, he knew he had to run as fast as his four legs would carry him. So that's exactly what he did.

As Pickle disappeared through the door, Wilma pulled herself up and wriggled into the vent. 'Whoever killed Visser,' she

panted, 'must have crawled down here to use the blow dart. So to find out who it was, all I have to do is follow the vent and find where it starts. This probably covers creeping after suspects, clue gathering AND being circuitous. Brilliant. I'm also behaving very seriously as well – top tip number nine. Mr Goodman will be pleased.'

The vent bent left and right and dipped downwards until it reached what looked like a blackened dead end, but as Wilma edged closer she realized that it turned upwards once more. Metal rungs were set into the bricks and with a bit of tricky negotiating Wilma was able to wiggle her way into a long, vertical shaft. The climb upwards was hard work, and the metal rungs were slimy with mould and lichen. Every now and again the light from the candle would pick out strange slug-like creatures that slithered in front of her but Wilma, determined not to scream or cry, because a proper, serious detective would never do that, stared only upwards and climbed on.

Wilma couldn't see much beyond the end of her candle, so when her head banged against what appeared to be a metal lid it was something of a surprise. Heaving the cover upwards, she pulled herself out from the shaft and, still on her hands and knees, held her candle aloft and looked about her. Through the gloom she made out that she was in the centre of a circle from which spiralled not one but five different tunnels. 'Which one shall I pick?' she mumbled to herself, as she spun on the spot. 'How do I know which is the right one?'

As she turned, holding out her candle to get a better look, her hands and knees sent up small clouds of dirt. She coughed, wafting a hand through the air. 'So dusty,' she spluttered, looking downwards. 'It's like crawling in snow. I'm leaving hand and footprints everywhere. Hang on! If I'm leaving a trail, then anyone else who was here must have left one too! If I find it and follow it, then I'll be able to pick the right tunnel!'

Bending down even further, she scoured the floor around, here and there, off to her right, were a set of scuffle marks that were not her own. Wilma was ecstatic. 'I must remember to tell Mr Goodman about this,' she said, grinning, as she crawled off in that direction. 'That's my best deduction yet!'

As she weaved left then right, the tunnel narrowed and the vents in the walls were smaller, but the ceiling began to get higher . . . until Wilma arrived at a dead end but was able to stand up at last. The marks just stop, she thought to herself, looking around with the candle. How can that be? You can't walk through walls.

Wilma placed a hand on the wall in front of her and ran her fingers over the surface, searching for an indent or a button or something out of the ordinary. She stood back and frowned. 'No secret button in front of me. Nothing to the sides,' she

pondered, tapping her bottom lip with a finger. 'How do I deduct myself out of this?'

Wilma stared up towards the ceiling and lifted the candle over her head. There, immediately above her, was a large metal hoop attached to a chain. Wilma smiled. With one small jump she grabbed hold of the hoop and pulled down. A deep, grating rumble shuddered from the wall in front of her as the bricks began to rearrange themselves, and to Wilma's astonishment a staircase gradually materialized in front of her very eyes. 'Wowzees,' she said, blinking hard. 'Can't wait to tell Pickle about this.'

The staircase wound away in a blind spiral. Wilma trod softly upwards and within moments she could see a hint of light. It was coming from a wooden door, and as Wilma climbed closer she could hear movement from the other side. Heart thumping, she placed a shaking hand against the door frame and pressed an eye to a thin gap in the wood. She was looking into what seemed to be a very plush office: there was a bookcase, a large bureau and just behind it a plinth-like structure with a miniature tree on it. Suddenly Wilma's view was obscured and, trying not to gasp, the brave ten-year-old realized that someone was standing in front of the door. If only she could see who it was! Peering as best she could, she caught sight of something that appeared to be furry. But what was it? Then the person on the other side of the door moved and suddenly everything became clear.

Standing with her back to Wilma was a woman with black hair tied up into a bun and a dark shawl wrapped around her shoulders. It looked like Miss Pagne! Wilma stood back again from the door. 'Miss Pagne?' she said quietly to herself. 'This must be the Museum! But how could the killer have started from here? Oh no! What if the killer is still here? I must warn her!'

Wilma lurched forward grabbed the door handle and burst into the room. 'Miss Pagne!' she shouted. 'You've got to get out of here! It's dangerous!'

As she yelled, Miss Pagne, whose back had stiffened, slowly turned around.

Wilma gasped and took a step backwards. 'But you're . . .' she said, backing into the wall behind her. 'I don't understand . . . the fingernail . . . it makes sense now . . . but it can't be! It can't . . .'

Sadly Wilma didn't get to finish her sentence. Because the heady smell of lavender laced with chloroform was already flooding her nostrils.

Told you it was going to get worse. Isn't this terrible?

CHAPTER 28

The fog had come down thick and without warning. Barbu D'Anvers, the island's most dastardly villain, was standing, cloak wrapped tight, with Janty immediately behind him. They had come to the Twelve Rats' Tails, the natural home of all Cooper's scallywags, with one thing on their minds: revenge.

'Can't see her anywhere, Mr Barbu,' said Tully, appearing from the mist.

'Nobody,' scowled Barbu, his jet-black hair flapping in the wind, 'tries to out-evil me. Tully, go inside and bring out Flatnose Detoit. Tell him I'd like a word.'

'Yes, Mr Barbu,' said the massive henchman. 'Shall I take the boy with me? To show him how it's done?'

Barbu turned and shot a glance in Janty's direction. 'I don't think so,' he said, narrowing his eyes a little. 'No self-respecting

228

scoundrel gets his own hands dirty. Let that be your second lesson, Janty. Always have a large stupid sidekick.'

Janty nodded. The cold wind blowing in over the harbour walls was spiking his cheeks crimson and, to keep warm, he pulled the sleeves of his jumper down over his hands. He knew what they had come to the docks to do and he had hardened his heart to it. They weren't just tracking down Barbu's rival; they were going to find whoever killed his father. And Janty wanted his own back.

'Here he is, Mr Barbu,' said Tully, galumphing out of the rickety inn door. Flatnose Detoit, the infamous island tittle-tattle, was tucked under Tully's arm like a roll of carpet, arms pinned to his sides.

'Flatnose,' Barbu began, pressing his mouth against the informant's ear, 'the last time we spoke, there was a woman. Tried to sell me lavender. Who is she?'

'N-n-no one knows, Mr D'Anvers,' said Flatnose, stuttering in terror, 'She always wears a hooded cloak. I wish I could help, but . . . owwww!'

Barbu rapped Flatnose's forehead with the silver head of his cane. 'What is the point,' he barked, nose to nose with the trapped rascal, 'of being an informant, if you are unable to inform? If you can't tell me who she is, then tell me where she is at least!'

'Oh!' said Flatnose, eyes widening. 'Well, you should have said. She was here not five minutes ago. Had a large sack over her shoulder. Went off in the direction of the docks.'

Barbu gritted his teeth. 'Then why didn't you tell me that in the first place, you idiot?' he yelled. 'Come on, Janty! Tully, shake him about a bit before you join us. Teach him a lesson.'

'I'd rather you didn't!' cried out Flatnose. 'I've just eaten a very heavy pie!' But Barbu and Janty were already pacing away into the fog, and as they disappeared from view Tully gave Detoit a good shake and then tossed him into a pile of broken bottles. 'Ohhhhhhh,' moaned the informant, holding his stomach and putting a hand to his mouth. 'I hate that!'

Theodore was scribbling furiously. Hunched over Visser's order book, he was deep in thought. 'I suppose the good thing about not knowing where Wilma is, is that whoever might be after her probably doesn't know either,' said Inspector Lemone, reaching for the plate of corn crumbles that Mrs Speckle had left for them.

'That's not what I'm worried about, Inspector,' said the great detective. 'Our problem isn't that the killer might find Wilma, it's that Wilma might find the killer. And then she'll be in all manner of trouble. Aha!' he added, triumphantly, thumping the order book with his fountain pen. 'As I suspected! Now I just need a couple more things . . .'

He reached into his bureau and pulled out a piece of paper. Writing on it with great speed he called out, 'Mrs Speckle! Can I have you, please?' Drying her hands on a knitted dishcloth, Mrs Speckle appeared in the doorway. She was wearing her knitted nightgown and double knitted slippers, and Inspector Lemone, who had never seen her in her bedroom attire before, gulped and went a bit quiet and solemn, the way gentlemen do when they're contemplating brand-new tyres.

'I'd like you to take this note to Captain Brock, please. And I want him to find Miss Pagne and arrest her.'

'About time!' spluttered Inspector Lemone.

Just then there was a bark from below the study window. Theodore jumped to his feet and flung the windows open. 'Pickle!' he shouted. 'Up you come, lad! Good boy!' Pickle leaped into the room and stood, tail wagging low and generally looking run ragged.

'There's a note in his collar!' cried out Inspector Lemone, pointing.

Theodore bent down to take it. 'What does it say, Goodman?' asked the Inspector, straining to look over the detective's shoulder. "Dear Mr Goodman. I have gone up the air vent to find clues." Oh no, Goodman. It's as we feared. She's taken matters into her own hands.'

'It's the worst news imaginable,' said Theodore, standing up

231

and crushing the note in his fist. 'If I'm right, and let's pray that I am, then we need to get to the docks this instant!'

'The docks?' shouted Inspector Lemone, running off after his friend for the second time that day. 'But what would she be doing at the docks?'

'It's not what she's doing at the docks, Inspector,' yelled Theodore, flinging open the cottage gate. 'It's what's being done to her! Mrs Speckle, when you see Captain Brock, have him do as I ask and meet me at dock number nine!'

'Saints preserve us,' panted Inspector Lemone, pacing to leap on the back of the tandem. 'Must get there in time! Just must!'

'Dock number nine,' repeated Mrs Speckle, in something of a fluster, as Theodore, the Inspector and Pickle disappeared from view. 'But what's happening at dock number nine?'

What indeed?

CHAPTER 29

Wilma was starting to come round. Too groggy to speak, she was vaguely aware that she was being carried in something rough to the touch like a coarse blanket or hessian sack. She wanted to wriggle herself free and put up some kind of fight, but her drugged body, heavy and lifeless, was unable to oblige. There was absolutely nothing she could do to help herself.

The air was cold and getting colder. Wilma felt herself being dropped to the ground and she lay motionless as someone above her wrestled with what sounded like a large sliding metal door. A blast of freezing air hit Wilma and the smell of fish filled her nostrils. Still unable to move, She could do nothing as the sack she was in was dragged heavily across the floor.

Suddenly the sack was swung back into the air, there was a flash of blinding light and Wilma felt herself being tumbled out from whatever she had been wrapped in. She

was in a brightly lit room but, still groggy, was unable to fully open her eyes. She could make out only indeterminate shapes: the shadowy person who loomed over her, dipping in and out of her line of vision, and a large block of trays or pallets stacked one on top of the other to her right.

Without the sack around her, Wilma was even colder. The chloroform had begun to wear off and, she was just able to curl herself into a tight ball for warmth.

'You have meddled for the last time, Wilma Tenderfoot,' said a voice, sounding thick and fuzzy as Wilma struggled to hear properly. 'Everyone who has stood in my way is now dead. Nosiness should never go unpunished. Didn't they teach you that at the Institute? Well, now you will learn it. And it will be the last lesson you ever learn!' An evil laugh punctured the air.

The figure moved away. Desperately Wilma tried to raise her head, but as she finally managed to pull herself up on to one elbow she heard a metal door being slammed sideways with a clatter. There was the click of an internal lock. The room was pitched into darkness.

'So . . . cold . . .' Wilma murmured, crawling forwards along the floor. She reached up to the stack of trays filled with fish to her right. If she could pull herself up, she thought, perhaps she could get to the door. She had to get out of this bitter chill. By now her breath was coming in short, sharp pants, billowing out n front of her in clouds of desperation. With every second that passed, she could feel her body seizing up. She was being frozen alive! If she didn't make it to the door, she would surely die!

She had managed to get one hand on the tray above her. Crying out, she pulled herself upwards. Now if she could just get to the door . . . but her legs weren't strong enough. Try as she might, Wilma couldn't move any further. This was it. These were her final moments.

Thoughts ran through her mind . . . Pickle . . . her first sight of Theodore P. Goodman . . . the luggage tag she'd earlier tied around her wrist . . . How faraway that all seemed now as she slumped slowly to the floor. And with those memories flashing through her thoughts, Wilma slipped into a dark, cold sleep from which there was little hope of return.

If you need a hanky, you might like to go and get one now.

CHAPTER 30

Theodore and Inspector Lemone were racing along the quay-side, Pickle hard on their heels. 'Not much further now,' panted the great detective. 'The old refrigeration unit is just ahead of us.'

'The place where they used to freeze all the fish?' gasped Inspector Lemone. 'Before they opened the new unit on the Farside.'

'That's right, Inspector!' shouted back Theodore. 'Pray we aren't too late!'

The island's original refrigeration unit was shrouded in the dense fog that had clouded in from the sea. As they ran towards its vast metal door, a lone bell rang on a buoy in the harbour like a death knell. Theodore and the Inspector grabbed hold of the weighty levered handle and heaved the sliding door aside.

It scraped open and a blast of freezing air exploded into their faces. 'A light!' Theodore shouted. 'Quickly!'

Inspector Lemone, hands shaking, reached up to a hook on the outside wall and lifted down a small lantern. Holding it in front of him, he swung it into the icy tomb, scanning the room frantically. 'There!' shouted Theodore, as the thin beam of light caught a small, huddled figure on the floor. Dashing towards her, Theodore ripped off his overcoat and, lifting Wilma into his arms, he wrapped her up as tightly as he could. 'Take off your coat, Inspector!' he yelled, as he carried Wilma out to the quay-side. 'We must get her warm!'

Lying Wilma on the ground, Theodore took the Inspector's coat and covered her with it. She was very pale, blue around the lips, and icy droplets had formed in her hair and eyebrows. 'She's not moving, Goodman,' murmured Inspector Lemone, voice catching in his throat. 'Please tell me we weren't too late.'

Theodore was rubbing her arms and legs as fast as he could. 'Must get the circulation going,' he said, with an intense frown. 'Come on, Wilma!' he urged. 'Don't give up on me now!'

Pickle leaned forward and gingerly began to lick Wilma's face. Still nothing happened. 'If only we'd been quicker,' Theodore whispered hopelessly – just as the plucky ten-year-old let out a small, dazed moan. Pickle stopped what he was doing and barked.

'Knew you wouldn't give up,' said the Inspector, a little choked.

Wilma's eyes opened slowly. 'The killer . . .' she began, struggling to speak. 'The vent . . . it's . . .'

'Don't worry about that, Wilma,' said Theodore, making sure the little girl was wrapped tight in the overcoats. 'Captain Brock has been waiting with his men. Whoever left this unit will be in his custody as we speak.'

'In fact, here he is, Goodman!' declared Inspector Lemone, standing up as Captain Brock approached through the gloom. 'And he's got the villain with him. I knew it! Miss Pagne! Just wanted the Katzin Stone to turn into some trinket, I should imagine! Well, I hope you're ashamed of yourself!'

Miss Pagne frowned at the Inspector. 'I have no idea what you're talking about,' she spluttered. 'And I'd like to know why I've been arrested! This is an outrage!'

'The brass of the woman!' exploded Inspector Lemone. 'You're the very worst sort of scorpion! Killing all those people. And now denying it! You're a proper poisoned pip!'

'Not so fast, Inspector,' said Theodore, placing a calming hand on his friend's back. 'Captain Brock, did you apprehend the person coming out from this unit?'

'I did, Mr Goodman,' said the Captain. 'Got your message from Mrs Speckle. Knew you'd want me to watch out for anything suspicious. So when I saw someone running off I sent two men to give chase. They'll have whoever it was back here in moments. In fact, I can hear them coming now.'

Everyone turned to peer through the fog. The outline of two soldiers appeared from the murky shadows and, between them, the hunched figure of a woman bent over a stick.

'Stand that person up, please,' said Theodore, touching his magnifying glass. 'And come into the light.'

'What the . . . ?' burst Inspector Lemone, shaking his head at what he saw. 'It can't be! It's another Miss Pagne! There are two of them!'

'No, Inspector,' said Theodore. 'Just someone dressed up to look like her. I apologize for having to have you arrested, Miss Pagne, but believe me when I say that is was for your own safety. Captain Brock, do the honours please. Let's unmask this rogue once and for all.'

Captain Brock stepped forward so that the hunched figure he now had hold of was standing immediately underneath the gaslight that burned on the quayside. Theodore stepped forward and grabbed a hold of the villains dark hair with his hand. 'Greed,' he said, pulling the wig off with a flourish, 'can indeed charm the greatest of men. Isn't that right, Mr Curator?'

'No!' gasped Inspector Lemone, shocked to his core. 'Well, I never!'

'And did you bring the other person I asked for, from the station, Captain Brock?' added Theodore, glancing sideways.

'I did, yes,' nodded the Captain. 'Step forward, Mrs Grimbles.'

A woman with white hair stepped into the light. She was old but sprightly, and had an air of authority about her. 'Mrs Grimbles,' said Theodore, shaking her hand, 'thank you for coming. I need your help. Tell me –' he gestured towards the Curator – 'do you recognize this man?'

'I do, yes,' she said, and with one outstretched finger she pointed towards him and added, 'He worked at my circus over twenty years ago as an odd-job man – until he left one day to make his fortune, and never came back. Left his poor wife heart-broken, the scoundrel. That is Fergus Waldock.'

'What the blue blazes!' declared Inspector Lemone, his brain in a spin.

'Thank you,' said the great detective, with a bow. 'I suspected as much. Visser's order book gave me the name, but I needed you to confirm that the Curator and Fergus Waldock were one and the same.'

Slowly the Curator raised his face into the light. 'I only made one mistake, Goodman,' he began, 'and that was underestimating you. And that meddling child!'

Inspector Lemone turned and shot Wilma a wink. 'Hear that,' he whispered. 'He means you.'

Wilma, still shivering, managed to muster a weak smile. Pickle gave her another lick.

'You were so desperate not to be discovered for who you really were that when you found out Wilma worked for Mrs Waldock – when you saw the photo she had of both of you – your great plan began to unravel,' said Theodore, standing tall and thrusting his thumbs into his waistcoat pockets. 'If you hadn't concerned yourself with her – and taken that same opportunity to get rid of Wilma – there is a chance that yes, you might have got away with it. But by going after someone so seemingly unconnected to the case, you gave me a huge clue. Though not your only one. From the beginning you have gone out of your way to hamper the investigation. The shard of poisoned sugar that you sent flying, leaving the feathered dart shaft on top of a corn crumble so that Pickle would eat it . . .'

'Terrible waste,' mumbled Inspector Lemone, shaking his head.

'Everything you did,' continued Theodore, 'was designed to destroy evidence and trip me up. Yes, it was you who commissioned Visser Haanstra to make the fake Katzin Stone, you who murdered Alan Katzin and his aunt so that you could disguise yourself as him, use his pass and switch the fake for the real thing using a simple sleight-of-hand trick taught to you all those years ago by your wife, Barbara Waldock. And the fake won you time to get back to the Museum and discover the stone missing. It was you who killed the forger who had helped you. Only he knew the truth, and so you eliminated him using a dart filled with poison made from the leaves of the Cynta tree in the arboretum that you pretended you knew nothing about. But in a picture in the paper taken on the day that Cynta tree was planted, there you were in the background, attending the ceremony as a guest – no doubt one with special access to the tree itself?! So when you denied all knowledge of it, at that moment I knew you were involved. But your greatest mistake was killing Mrs Waldock. You were getting clumsy and by leaving the body of a known skinflint in front of an open fire I finally understood how you had been killing your victims.'

'Oh good,' said Inspector Lemone. 'I've been waiting for this bit.'

'Your method was fiendish,' said Theodore, fingering his magnifying glass. 'You began with stealth, creeping up on your victims and pretending to offer them lavender. But the lavender was infused with chloroform, drugging them instantly so that you could drag them here, to the abandoned refrigeration unit. You left them to freeze to death and then, so as not to arouse suspicion, you took the bodies back to their homes, where you left them to defrost. That was why there were no marks on the bodies. And why their hearts were still frozen!'

'Because they weren't quite thawed through!' shouted Wil-

ma, who was slowly reviving. 'That's why we found that fish scale too!'

'Devilish clever!' commented the Inspector, shaking his head.

'But not clever enough, Inspector Lemone,' said Theodore. 'And on top of that, you tried to frame your assistant. You disguised yourself as her, perhaps you even hoped the red fingernail left on Mrs Waldock's body or Miss Pagne's love of trees would lead us to her – but anyone can see Miss Pagne's fine set of fingernails are entirely real.'

'Despicable fellow!' growled the Inspector. 'Blaming a woman like that!'

'I don't know what to say,' muttered Miss Pagne, who was clearly in shock. 'Except . . . I resign!'

'Resignation accepted!' spat the Curator. 'All you ever did was flirt with every Tom and Johnny-Jack that came into the office! But did you ever pay me any attention? Never!'

'Unrequited love,' explained the Inspector with a small sigh.

'Not love,' sneered the Curator. 'I learned that lesson a long time ago. She's just like my wife – so busy fluttering her glamorous-assistant eyelashes at everyone, an errand boy like me barely had a look in even though we were married. So I set off to find my own fortune and I ended up at the Museum, surrounded by its beautiful things – and for a while that was enough. At night, once the doors were closed, it was almost as if they were mine, all mine. But they weren't, not really – and then the Katzin Stone came along. I saw its picture before it was due to arrive. It was so big, so beautiful, so utterly priceless – I had to have it, to keep it for myself. I wanted the whole of Cooper to know what it was like to see something beautiful, then have it taken away . . . forever . . . !' His voice faded away on this last line and he turned his face back into the shadows.

'So where's the Katzin Stone now?' asked Wilma, trying to sit up. 'Seeing as that was the start of everything.'

'Here,' said a voice, emerging from behind them. It was Barbu D'Anvers, flanked by Tully and Janty. 'And under International Finders Keepers rules, I don't have to give it back.'

CHAPTER 31

'He can't be allowed to get away with that!' cried out Wilma, leaning on Pickle for support.

'I'm afraid he's right,' said Theodore. 'Finders Keepers does mean that a person who locates anything that's gone missing is allowed to hold on to it.'

'I must say,' said Barbu, with a triumphant sneer, 'I have been enjoying listening to everything. Most illuminating.'

'Is that the man who killed my father?' spat Janty, his grey eyes flashing at the Curator.

'I'm afraid it is,' answered Theodore, adopting a serious tone. 'And I can promise you that he will be brought to justice.'

'I'll punish him myself!' shouted Janty and, pulling a small pistol from his pocket, he aimed it at the Curator. The Curator, seeing the raised gun, screamed and cowered with fear.

'No, Janty!' cried out Wilma, struggling to her feet. 'Two wrongs don't make anything right!'

Janty paused and, glancing at Wilma, something in him faltered. Theodore, seeing an opportunity, threw himself forward and knocked the gun from the small boy's hand.

'Best not to do anything you'll regret,' he said, picking up the gun.

Barbu turned and stared at his young charge. 'Never,' he began, with a frown, 'try and shoot anyone in front of police officers. Honestly. That's just basic. Anyway, where did you get that?'

'I made it,' snarled Janty, kicking at the ground.

'Hmmm,' replied Barbu, raising an eyebrow. 'Impressive.'

'It's not me you should want to kill anyway!' shouted the Curator, wild-eyed. 'Why don't you ask your new master what he was doing to your father before I put him out of his misery?'

'Ah ha ha,' laughed Barbu, a little nervously. 'Never mind him, Janty. He's rambling. It's what everyone does when they've been caught. He's desperate. Don't even look at him. It's too sad.'

'What do you mean?' asked the boy, staring back at the Curator.

'Ask him why your father was beaten before he was killed! Who did that to him? It wasn't me! It was him – and his stupid thug.'

Janty turned to glare at his master. 'Is this true? Did you hurt my father?'

'He did!' yelled Wilma. 'Honestly — he's awful! You should stay away from him!'

'Oh, do you ever shut up?' moaned Barbu, rolling his eyes. 'All right. Technically we might have tortured your father. But only for a bit! Let's not bog down the issue with facts! I'm evil! This is what I do! I mean — so what? What are you going to do? Put me on the naughty step? Give me a Chinese burn? And I only gave him a little roughing up. He was a forger! It goes with the territory! Come on!'

Janty's lips tightened. 'You didn't kill him, I suppose . . .'

'Exactly!' exclaimed Barbu, throwing his arms up. 'So can we move on? Thank you! Let's get down to business. I've got the Katzin Stone, and with it I'm going to buy the island. And my first decree, when I own everywhere, is having you sacked, Goodman!'

'It's not worth anything, Barbu,' said Theodore, handing Janty's homemade pistol to Captain Brock.

'Don't be ridiculous,' laughed Barbu, reaching for the stone in his pocket and holding it aloft. 'It's practically priceless!'

'No, it's worthless,' repeated Theodore, turning to face his nemesis. 'Because it's not the real Katzin Stone. Pickle, fetch!'

Pickle leaped up at the command and, before Barbu could react, snatched the stone from the villain's hand in his mouth.

248

Dropping it from his mouth into the detective's lowered palm, he returned to a wide-mouthed Wilma's side.

'I believe that, at the Curator's request, Visser made two fake stones,' explained Theodore. 'One to be placed in the original casket and the other to act as a decoy should the investigation threaten to tighten its net. The Curator's next step would have been to place the decoy – left with Visser for safekeeping, no doubt – on Miss Pagne, and have us find her with it! Barbu, you must have found the decoy before the Curator could pick it up to use it. And to prove it's worthless, if I drop the stone into that small puddle of water then . . .' Everyone watched in amazement as the sugar-based gem fizzed and disappeared. 'It simply melts.'

'Then where is the REAL one?' screamed Barbu, clouting Janty about the ears.

'I'll never tell,' wailed the Curator, both hands clutching the top of his cane as he leaned heavily upon it.

'No need,' continued Theodore, also taking hold of the Curator's cane. 'It was right in front of our noses all along. Here, set in the end of the Curator's cane!'

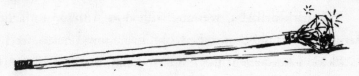

'Oh!' screamed Barbu, livid. 'That is so sneaky! If you're going to be evil,' he shouted, in the Curator's direction, 'at least be honest about it!'

'Well, blow me down!' said Inspector Lemone, scratching his head. 'If you haven't done it again, Goodman!'

'Yes, well,' replied Theodore, with a small, satisfied twiddle of his moustache. 'It took me quite a while to work out that code. But as soon as I had, everything fell into place. And I must say, we have Wilma to thank for bringing it to me. Credit where it's due and all that.'

'Here, here!' echoed the Inspector, with a grin. 'Yes, well,' he added, suddenly becoming quite stern, 'I suppose that leaves me to conclude the official business. Take the Curator to jail, Captain Brock. Dressing up like an innocent woman indeed. Stealing stones. Killing aunts. I'll be surprised if you ever see the light of day again!'

'You've not heard the last of me, Inspector!' yelled the Curator as he was dragged away. 'One day I shall own all the treasures on the island! I'm the greatest criminal mind on Cooper!'

'No!' barked Barbu, seething with rage. 'I think you'll find that's ME! Any old hootenanny can hide a jewel on the end of a stick! Think yourself lucky you're going to jail! If I'd got to you first it would be a VERY different story! And as for you,

250

Theodore P. Goodman, you may have won this time, but I shall be back! You can depend on it! Tully! Janty!' And with the usual sweep of his cloak, Barbu and his two companions vanished into the fog.

Wilma watched with concern as Janty disappeared from view. 'I'm sure there's good in that boy,' she said, with a small shake of her head. 'He just needs to get away from that awful Barbu D'Anvers. Talking of which, shouldn't we try and catch him or something?' she continued, looking puzzled. 'He's SUCH a dreadful man.'

'The day for dealing with Barbu D'Anvers will come soon enough, Wilma,' answered Theodore, scooping the little girl up. 'Now then, Inspector Lemone, I'd be grateful if you could escort Miss Pagne home. I'm only sorry,' he said, turning to the secretary, 'that you had to go through this.'

'Yes,' mumbled the Inspector, looking very contrite. 'Sorry for calling you a poisoned pip and everything.'

'That's all right,' replied Miss Pagne, wrapping her shawl tighter about her. 'I can see why you thought it was me. Especially when he was in disguise. Although I'd like to think I have much better ankles.'

'Well, that's that,' said Theodore. 'That concludes the case. I think we should get this young lady back to Clarissa Cottage and a warm bath.'

'And some corn crumbles, Goodman?' asked Inspector Lemone.

'Capital idea!' answered Theodore. 'And maybe even a good game of Lantha!'

'Well, prepare to be beaten,' added Wilma as she was carried away, 'because I am VERY determined.' And Pickle barked his agreement.

The Curator, eh? Let that be a lesson to you all. NEVER trust a fat man with a cane.

CHAPTER 32

'All right,' said Wilma, holding Visser's order book open, 'I'll explain it the way Mr Goodman explained it to me. But if you don't get it this time, Pickle, then I'm afraid you'll have to give up. So in the picture at the top, there are two sculptures of cats. Two cats. Made out of stone. So that's cats in stone. Katzin Stone. Get it? Then comes the name. Here's the picture of the animal hide. That's FUR. Then there's the picture of the beaker with the vapour coming out of it. So that's GAS. Then the square of bricks. Obviously that's WALL. And what do you need when you sting your hand with a nettle? No need to answer. I'll tell you. It's a dock leaf. So that's FUR-GAS WALL-DOCK. Then there are the numbers. And if you take the alphabet and give every letter a numerical value with 1 starting at Z and working backwards to A which is 26, then it spells out . . . Can you guess it, Pickle? It's FERGUS

WALDOCK. So that's how he knew it was him. Simple really.'

It took Wilma two days to recover from her ordeal, and despite being weakened and under the weather it was the happiest she had ever been. Tucked into a large marshmallow bed and leaning up against soft feather pillows, Wilma was waited on hand and foot. Mrs Speckle brought her meals on a tray, Detective Goodman popped in every day at corn-crumble time to check on his young friend, and Pickle, exhausted by their joint efforts, never left her side. It was lazy and restful – exactly what the pair of them needed, and as the sun streamed in through the bedroom window Wilma could only marvel at how perfect everything seemed to be.

'Knock, knock!' said a familiar voice at the bedroom door. Inspector Lemone poked his head into view. 'Thought I'd come and see the patient! How are you?'

Wilma grinned. 'Hello, Inspector Lemone,' she said. 'Much better, thank you. I might even get up today.'

'So,' said the Inspector, sitting down on the edge of Wilma's bed, 'I thought you'd like to see something. Something you might like to put on that Clue Ring of yours.'

'Something for my Clue Ring?' asked Wilma, excited. 'What is it?'

'Why don't you have a look for yourself?' said the Inspec-

tor, with a wink. Reaching into the pocket of his overcoat, he pulled out the late-morning newspaper and tore out an article. 'There you go,' he added, handing it to Wilma. 'Have a read of that.'

Wilma took the paper, unfolded it and read, '"The Case of the Frozen Hearts – final analysis"? But that's the case I worked on!' Wilma stared up at the Inspector, her eyes wide and bright. 'It's in the paper! Like all the other things on my Clue Ring!'

'That's right!' laughed Inspector Lemone, slapping his knee. 'And look there! A picture of you and Pickle!'

Wilma couldn't believe her eyes. 'But only great detectives like Mr Goodman get their pictures in the paper!' she said, mouth agape.

'Well, there you are,' insisted the Inspector, tapping the paper with his finger. 'I guess that must mean you're a great detective!'

'Don't be silly,' said Wilma, shoving the Inspector in the arm. 'Not yet! But perhaps one day I will be. Now I've had my picture in the paper and everything.'

'Perhaps one day you will,' nodded Inspector Lemone. 'Ooooh, is that a plate of corn crumbles? Mind if I have one?'

Wilma stared at the news clipping in front of her and smiled. She had never felt so proud in her life. Making a little hole in its top right-hand corner, she took her Clue Ring and slipped it on. 'Imagine that, Pickle,' she whispered, giving her beagle a little

rub around the ears. 'You and me actually on the Clue Ring! Things don't get better than that.'

You might be thinking that this would be a good place to finish the story because the case has been solved, the villain caught and Wilma isn't dead. In fact, it's safe to say that everything seems to have turned out positively rosy. Under normal circumstances this would be an excellent place to just say 'The End', and everyone could go about their business, but we're all forgetting one thing: Madam Skratch. Wilma, lest we forget, only days ago escaped from the Institute for Woeful Children, thus breaking just about every rule in that establishment's book. And as Wilma was enjoying her small moment of triumph, Madam Skratch was pulling up in her blackened cart outside Clarissa Cottage for the second and last time.

Mrs Speckle, who had answered the door, because that was her job, was wringing water out of a knitted tea towel and looking out from underneath the brim of her bobble hats. 'Can I help you?' she asked, as Madam Skratch stood scowling on the front porch. 'Because we don't need any sponges or cleaning cloths, so if you're selling, I'm not interested.'

Madam Skratch looked down her nose at the woollen-clad housekeeper and sucked in her cheeks. 'How dare you! I am the matron of the Institute for Woeful Children! As you well know!

Anyway, I read in the paper that Wilma Tenderfoot is back here. And she is my property. So I have come for her. I should have known she'd end up back here when that annoying detective man came looking for her the day she escaped,' she said, in a pinched tone. 'Please tell her to get her things immediately.'

Mrs Speckle, who was not known for her impeccable manners, clacked her lips and thought about that. She was quite keen to say something very rude indeed to the unwelcome guest standing on the porch of Clarissa Cottage, but sadly everyone had been painfully aware that this moment was inevitable. Without an apprenticeship or a job to go to on the Farside, Wilma would have to go back and that was that. And Wilma most definitely did NOT have an apprenticeship – Detective Theodore P. Goodman wasn't even in to say goodbye.

Wilma, who had very little to call her own, was, after she had got dressed and tucked her few bits and pieces into her pinafore pocket, ready to return to her former miserable life. As she approached Madam Skratch's cart at the gate, she gave a last look over her shoulder in case anyone special was returning just in time to save her – but there was no one there. So she bent down and held on to Pickle for the longest time. 'I love you, Pickle,' she whispered, at which point Inspector Lemone, who had been gulping non-stop from the moment he'd clapped eyes on

Madam Skratch, had to turn away and pretend he'd got a considerable amount of dust in his eyes. Pickle gazed mournfully at his friend from whom he was about to be parted and did what a dog sometimes has to do: he howled.

As the little girl heaved herself on to the back of the cart Mrs Speckle stepped forward and pressed a small box into Wilma's hands. 'Just a few corn crumbles,' she said with a nod, 'because I know you like them and, well . . .' But even Mrs Speckle couldn't finish her sentence, and she too had to lower her head and think very hard about something that wasn't remotely heartbreaking.

'Thank you,' Wilma whispered. With one last glance at the empty path she gave a sad smile, then turned and put a hand on the Inspector's shoulder. 'Inspector Lemone,' she said, looking into his eyes when he raised his tear-stained gaze, 'I just wanted to say that I think you're one of the kindest, bravest men I could ever hope to know. I'm very glad I met you.'

'And I'm very glad I met you too,' answered the Inspector, eyes filling up again. 'Actually, I don't think I'll bother with the gulping now, if that's all right with you.' And he got his handkerchief out and gave way to a heaving sob.

'Driver!' barked Madam Skratch, who had also got back into the cart. 'Return us to the Institute. Quick as you can!'

Wilma spun round and grabbed the matron's forearm.

258

'Please,' she begged, 'can't we stay just a little longer? I haven't said goodbye to Detective Goodman!'

'Yes,' piped up Inspector Lemone, wiping his eyes. 'Where is the fellow?'

'I am here, Inspector,' called out Theodore, who was running towards the cart from up the road. 'And I have with me a piece of paper that I'd like Madam Skratch to take a look at!'

'Oh, what now?' said the cheerless matron, rolling her eyes. 'I really don't have time for any more of this nonsense.'

'This isn't nonsense, Madam Skratch,' said Theodore, with a wry smile. 'I think you'll find this is very serious indeed.' Reaching into his overcoat pocket, Theodore pulled out an official-looking document. 'Have a read of that, Matron! I think it changes everything.'

Madam Skratch took the paper. Muttering and mumbling about inconveniences and time wasting, she began to read. 'But this can't be,' she said, after a moment looking up. 'Are you quite mad?'

'Not in the least, Madam,' answered Theodore, getting out his pipe and popping it into his mouth.

'Well, what is it?' wailed the Inspector. 'I can't bear the tension!'

'It's a Contract of Apprenticeship,' Madam Skratch said with a stunned expression. 'Detective Goodman has taken Wilma as his apprentice.'

259

Wilma's mouth fell open and her eyes grew as large as saucers. 'But . . .' she stuttered, shaking her head in disbelief, 'that can't be true . . . it's too good to be true . . . is it true? Am I dreaming? I get to stay? And make deductions every day?'

'It is true, Wilma!' laughed Theodore, reaching up and lifting the little girl out of the cart. 'And you'll live here at Clarissa Cottage with me and Mrs Speckle.'

'That's just . . . lovely . . .' sobbed the Inspector, tears streaming down his cheeks.

'I can't believe it,' said Wilma, surrounded by her friends. 'I never belonged anywhere and I never had a family. And now, I sort of have.'

Madam Skratch, who was quietly livid that the girl had got her own way, arched her back. 'Actually,' she sneered, 'that's not quite true. There is a member of Wilma's family still alive.'

The words fell like a bombshell. Wilma turned, her eyes widened in disbelief. '*Because they gone,*' she whispered, fumbling in her pinafore pocket for the luggage tag. 'But who is it?' she asked, gripping Madam Skratch's arm. 'And where are they?'

'How should I know?' Madam Skratch barked, swatting Wilma's hand from her black sleeve. 'All I know is that I got money to keep you about! What do I care where your family are? That's something you'll have to find out for yourself. Driver, the Institute!'

*

As Madam Skratch rattled away in her jet-black cart, Wilma, Pickle, Detective Theodore P. Goodman, Inspector Lemone and Mrs Speckle could do nothing but stand in shock. Somewhere Wilma had a relative. They were all so baffled that it was a few moments before anyone spoke. 'Well!' said Mrs Speckle finally, shoving up the sleeves of her woollen cardigan. 'That was a surprise. And the best thing I know for sudden moments is a pot of peppermint tea and a plate of corn crumbles!'

'Better make that plate a big one, Mrs Speckle,' said the Inspector, scratching his head. 'In fact, I'll come and help you carry it . . . if you'd like me to.'

Mrs Speckle scrunched her nose up under her bobble hats and thought about that. 'All right then,' she said with a shrug, and waddled off. Inspector Lemone beamed. This was fast turning into the best day of his life.

Wilma spun round to face Theodore. 'But how will I find whoever it is, Mr Goodman? I don't know how to do it.'

Theodore looked down, put a hand on Wilma's back and took a puff on his pipe. 'It won't be easy,' he began, 'but where do all detectives begin?'

'With clues and deductions,' answered Wilma, eyes brightening.

'Just so.' Theodore nodded, steering his young apprentice up the garden path of Clarissa Cottage. 'And if anyone can do it, we can.'

'Nothing and no one stops Wilma Tenderfoot,' said Wilma, with a determined nod. 'The thing is, Mr Goodman, I've got this luggage tag . . .'

Now that's the end. Or is it?

To be continued . . .

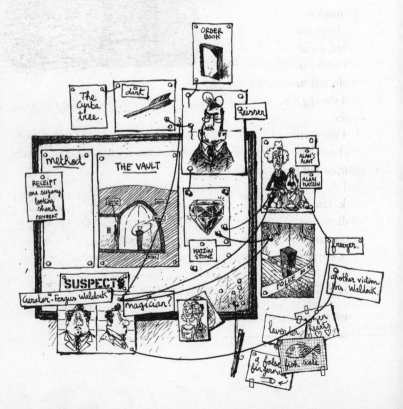

CORN CRUMBLES

NOW YOU CAN ENJOY COOPER ISLAND'S FAVOURITE BISCUIT

Makes about 30

Method

1. Preheat the oven to 180 °C, gas mark 4.
2. In a large bowl, cream the butter, sugar and lemon zest with a metal spoon or an electric hand-mixer
3. Add the egg and use a wooden spoon or the mixer to form a lumpy batter.
4. Add the cornmeal and flour a couple of tablespoons at a time until you have a dough dry enough to roll out. You might need a bit more flour, or not quite this much.
5. Roll the dough out on a clean, floured surface until it's about ¾ cm thick. Use a small round cutter (about the size of an eggcup), or cut small squares or triangles with a knife, to make small biscuits. Then roll out any spare dough again until you've used it all.
6. Place the biscuits at least two centimetres apart on a baking sheet and bake for 18 to 20 minutes, until golden brown.
7. Allow to cool before eating – if you can wait!

Serve with peppermint tea or your favourite drink.

YOU WILL NEED

100 g butter, soft

100 g castor sugar

zest of 1 lemon (wash the lemon, then, with a fine grater, grate the yellow outside only)

1 egg, beaten

100 g polenta (cornmeal – fine or coarse, it doesn't matter)

150 g plain flour

¼ tsp salt

2 large baking sheets, lightly oiled

Look out for . . .

Wilma Tenderfoot
THE CASE of
THE Putrid POISON

A threatening note.
A bucket.
Some poisonous foam.

It sounds like ANOTHER case for
Wilma Tenderfoot

Coming soon!